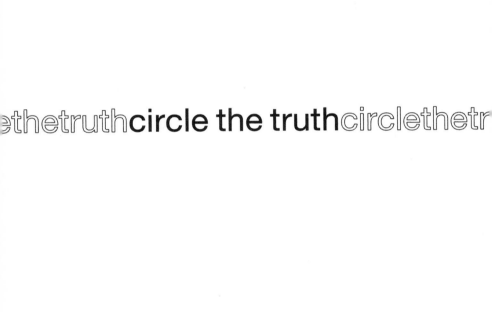

uthcirclethetruthcirclethetruthcirc

ethetruthcircle the truthcirclethetr

PAT SCHMATZ

CAROLRHODA BOOKS, INC.   MINNEAPOLIS • NEW YORK

I have tremendous gratitude for the Minnesota children's writing community, especially the Jane Resh Thomas group and the Hayward group. I also appreciate the help from Ruth Schmatz, Robin Stevenson, Dalton Savage, and the Pediatric Emergency Medicine staff at Children's Hospital in Minneapolis. Thanks to my editor, Shannon Barefield, and particular thanks for the patience and keen eye of my agent, Andrea Cascardi. –P.S.

Carolrhoda Books, Inc.
A division of Lerner Publishing Group, Inc.
241 First Avenue North
Minneapolis, MN 55401

Website address: www.lernerbooks.com

Library of Congress Cataloging-in-Publication Data

Schmatz, Pat.
    Circle the Truth / by Pat Schmatz
       p. cm.
    Summary: Eighth-grader Orithian "Rith" Haley discovers another world via the staircase in his house and begins to explore questions about God and about the father he never knew.
     ISBN: 978–0–8225–7268–8 (lib. bdg. : alk. paper)
     [1. Fathers—Fiction. 2. Spiritual Life—Fiction. 3. Space and time—Fiction.] I. Title.
    PZ7.S34734Ci 2007
    [E]—dc22
                                          2006101327

Manufactured in the United States of America
1 2 3 4 5 6 –BP– 12 11 10 09 08 07

To *Jane Resh Thomas*
and
In Memory of Auntie Babbitt

Both persistent circlers of truth   .

The feeling reached into Rith's dreamless sleep, where he was slouching around in the never-changing mud of boredom and hopelessness. It yanked him into the gray-dark bedroom and left him lying jittery awake, shifting his wide-open eyes without moving his head. It paced around the edge of his bed, invisible but tangible. It slithered under the sheets and Rith's skin broke out in goose bumps.

He panicked and flipped to his side, groping for the light. His hand hit a glass of water that sloshed and clattered on the nightstand, then thumped on the carpet. He found the lamp and grabbed the stem with one hand, hitting the switch with the other. With a click and a flash, light entered the room and the feeling left.

Nothing and nobody, just his stupid imagination.

Rith got up and searched the room, mocking himself the whole time. What do you think, there's a monster in the closet? Maybe a wizard on a broomstick outside the window? A python under your bed? He picked up the water glass and used yesterday's sock to wipe water off the nightstand. Most of it was already soaking into the thick blue carpet. He pressed his ear against the closed bedroom door, listening for sounds in the hall that he knew wouldn't be there.

He got back in bed and turned off the light, lying in the darkness. The streetlight wavered through the plaid curtains and glanced off the blank computer screen on his desk. The TV on top of the dresser hulked in the deepest shadows of the corner.

Rith kicked the covers away. His stepfather, Walt, kept the house way too hot.

"Babies in the house," he'd say. "Gotta keep things cozy."

He and Mom and the babies were a long way away, down on the first floor. The nursery where Ben and Emma slept was next to the huge master bedroom. That bedroom, with its attached bathroom and walk-in closet, was bigger than the whole house where Rith had lived with his mom B.W. Before Walt.

If something really did sneak into Rith's window in the night and attack him, no one would know. They wouldn't hear a thing. Mom would come looking for him when he didn't show up at breakfast and find him spattered all over the room, maggots crawling around in whatever was left of him. Or maybe he'd disappear without a trace. They'd come in and find his window left open, cold air rushing in. Walt would be outraged that something had dared break into his castle and touch one of his subjects without permission. Mom might be sad for a week or two, but then she'd say, "Can't we forget about the past and focus on the good things we have now?" And then she'd live happily ever after.

The next morning, Rith lifted his heavy eyelids to watch the sky lighten. First everything was gray, and then a lighter gray, then the sun began to shine its feeble rays across the winter sky. The branches on the trees were long naked tentacles, reaching up in search of warmth.

The posters on the walls slowly came clear—Harry Potter, Eragon, and Redwall. Fantasy stuff, dragons and broomsticks and mouse warriors. Water ran somewhere in the house but no other sounds reached Rith. On non-school days, he put off an appearance on the ground floor as long as possible.

"Rit!" Emma's voice floated up from the living room below.

She sang his name, making a rhythm of it as she crawled up the stairs. Rith put on a pair of sweats and a tee shirt and opened the door. Emma's voice paused on the landing, then continued. Her curly head poked around the corner.

Her eyes widened when she saw him and she laughed out loud. She ran over and threw her sturdy little blonde self at his legs, making him put his hand against the wall to keep from falling over.

"Hi, Emma," he said.

She squealed and let loose with an unintelligible stream of sounds. Emma bubbled noise every minute she was

9

awake. She didn't care if Rith glared at her, closed doors on her, or pretended she didn't exist. He got almost as much air time as "Daddy Daddy Daddy."

The only way to get rid of her was to go downstairs with her.

"Come on," he said. "Let's go find some food."

She clutched a handful of loose material behind Rith's left knee and followed him down the hall. When Rith reached the top of the stairs, they stretched out before him, wide and covered with thick, soft no-color carpeting.

Rith picked Emma up and put her under his arm like a football. He carried her down the stairs, her head bobbing and her feet flopping behind. At the bottom he set her down and followed the slap of her bare feet across the big, square ceramic tiles into the sunny kitchen.

"Rit," she announced to her parents, beaming as if she had discovered gold on the second floor.

"Good morning, hon," said Rith's mother. She sat at the table with Baby Ben, who lounged in her lap like a fat little prince, sucking away on his bottle.

"How'd you sleep?" she asked.

"Fine," said Rith, rummaging through the cupboard for the Frosted Flakes.

"Hey Sugar," boomed Walt, taking Emma up on his lap. "How's your big brother this morning?"

Rith poured the Frosted Flakes into a bowl, pulled the milk out of the refrigerator and splashed it on, and started to head upstairs.

"Rith," said Walt. "Did you forget something?"

He stopped and rolled his eyes at the wall in front of him. He sighed, backtracked, rolled up the lining of the cereal box and returned it to the cupboard, and put the milk back in the refrigerator. Then, without looking at anyone, he picked up his bowl and headed back to his room.

Upstairs, Rith sat at his desk and ate his cereal, looking out the window. Not much to see on an icy gray morning. Big houses like their house, sitting around the circular end of the street. All the driveways neatly snow-blown, all the SUVs shut up in their garages. He looked down at the snow just outside the window, pressing his face against the cold glass. To his left, the back yard stretched out into an open field between their house and the next identical cul-de-sac. He searched for footprints or paw prints or maybe a secret symbol drawn in the snow. Some sign that the feeling he'd had in the night was more than a wild wishful hope for a break from reality.

There was nothing. Nothing and nobody. Just another stupid Sunday morning.

Two hours later, Rith waited by the coat rack because that was better than standing in the church doorway with Walt and Mom and the babies, shaking the hands of everyone as they walked in. Helping ladies off with their coats was painful but not unbearable.

"Hey." Someone tapped Rith on the shoulder.

He turned to face a pudgy kid a little taller than him with red hair and lots of freckles.

"I'm Toby."

"Hi. I'm Rith."

"What?" asked Toby, like everyone did.

"Rith. Short for Orithian."

"Rrrrrrrrith," Toby growled. "Cool name. Not like Toby. Toby sounds like an overweight beagle. Why couldn't they have named me Brutus or Spike, like a pit or a rott?"

"Hi Rith," called Mrs. Hughes, shrugging out of her long wool coat. "So nice to see you, and how's that darling little sister of yours?"

"She's fine," said Rith, although all Mrs. Hughes had to do was turn around and see for herself. He took her coat and put it on a hanger.

"So you're the coat man here?" asked Toby as Mrs. Hughes walked away. "How'd you get that job?"

"Greeter family," said Rith, pointing toward the entrance with his head. "It's either shake hands or hang coats. I hang coats. Want to help?"

"Sure thing," said Toby, glancing over at the Kurths. "Where'd you get that name, anyway?" he asked. "O-rith-i-an."

"Family name, from my dad."

"Sounds like you oughta be pals with Eragon. You read that?"

"Yeah, great book," said Rith, taking another coat.

Toby stepped in and helped Mrs. Johanson, who was so teeny-tiny that her coat probably weighed more than she did. The flurry of people grew and for a few minutes, both boys took and hung coats as fast as they could. Then the crowd started to thin, and Toby followed Rith to the rack with a last jacket.

"So this church business," he said. "I'm new here. Are there, like, assigned pews or something? Or do you just sit wherever?"

"Wherever," said Rith. "Your parents here?"

"Nope. They were bad so I left them home." Toby grinned. "Can I sit with you?"

"If you want," said Rith. "I have to sit with them though." He jerked his head again toward the doorway.

Mom and Walt were just leaving their post to take the babies down to the nursery.

"Mom, this is Toby," called Rith. "He's going to sit with us, okay?"

"Sure, that's fine." Mom smiled. "You boys go ahead and sit down while we get the kids settled. We'll be right in."

"Wow, your dad must be half giant," said Toby, as Mom and Walt went downstairs.

"Not my dad," said Rith as they headed into the church sanctuary. "That's just Walt."

The ushers handed them church bulletins and Rith led the way down the center aisle to the usual pew.

"Do you come every week?" Toby whispered as Rith pulled his sermon notes from his back pocket.

Rith nodded, unfolding the paper and printing his name at the top: *Orithian Haley.* He started filling it in, copying the Bible references for the day from the church bulletin. Toby reached over and tapped Rith's last name.

"Very comet-ish," he whispered. "What's that you're writing?"

"For confirmation class," said Rith. "Gotta turn it in after church."

Mom and Walt slid into the pew just as the organ started. Walt leaned over and gave Rith the eye, and then glanced at Toby. Just in case Rith was planning on having fun for once, but that was a wasted worry. Toby did everything Rith did, watching him for cues of when to sit and stand. He followed along in the bulletin, listened to the service, and flipped through the hymnal ahead of time to get on the right page. He even sang along on the hymns, which Rith refused to do.

After the benediction, Toby turned to Rith and said, "So do you go to Franklin?"

"Yup, eighth grade," said Rith.

"Me too," said Toby. "I'm new this year. We just moved last summer. I'm in the Spanish immersion program up on the third floor, so I'm not in regular classes. I'll look for you in the hall though."

"Okay," said Rith. "Slide out that way or we'll be stuck here forever."

Rith looked back over his shoulder as he and Toby slid out to the side aisle. Mom was talking to a couple of other women. He caught her eye and pointed at Toby. She nodded and went back to talking. Toby followed Rith as he dropped off his sermon notes in the envelope by the door. They slipped around the pastor-greeting traffic jam and into the foyer.

"I gotta get outside," said Toby. "My dad'll be waiting. He'll be afraid I got kidnapped and brainwashed in here."

"Really?" asked Rith. "Why?"

"He says church is—" Toby stood up straight and deepened his voice—"shot through with hypocrisy. So I better get out there and show him I'm okay. See you."

Toby grabbed his jacket and trotted down the steps, turning back to wave. Rith helped some of the older people find coats and get them on. Everyone chitchatted and milled around on their way out. The front door opened and closed, letting in puffs of icy air. Once most everyone was gone, Rith pulled his jacket off the hanger and went down the few steps to the door, leaning his forehead against the window. The sun was trying to break through but the clouds wouldn't give up. They smeared a wispy film over it, muting the light and heat.

Mom and Walt were taking an awfully long time to collect the kids. Between the bundling-up and shoe-tying and carseat-fastening and greeting and coat-hanging, they spent half the day coming to and going from church. Wasted time—except for meeting Toby. Church was the last place he'd expected to find a kid who'd read *Eragon*, much less one who appreciated the cometness of his name.

B.W., Mom had wanted to go to some churches just for fun. See if they'd be nice to the heathens, she'd said. But her whole heathen thing dropped pretty fast once she met Walt. Rith said the prayers and dropped money in the offering plate but he was still a heathen. If it was good enough for his dad, it was good enough for him.

"Rith."

Her hand on his shoulder.

"Nice that you made a friend here. Will he be in confirmation class, too?"

Rith shrugged, looking out in the direction where Toby had disappeared.

"Come and help me bring the kids upstairs. Walt stopped off to talk with Pastor."

He didn't really mean to shake his head no again—his head did the shaking all by itself. Her hand dropped away. He didn't need to see her face to know the look on it. He was the only thing that ever made her unhappy anymore.

"Please, Rith. Don't be like that."

The words were like a thick heavy rope knotting around his neck, cutting off the last breath of the good feeling he'd gotten from Toby. Just like the clouds moving over the sun. He shoved his hands in his pockets, turned, and trudged with her down the stairs toward the nursery.

Monday night something thumped on the stairs, jerking Rith awake. He stared into the darkness, listening. He barely breathed, just a little air in and out through his mouth.

Thump! Again, like something soft landing on a hard floor. Rith's heart crashed around inside his chest. Not nothing this time, not making it up. Something was really out there. Slowly, slowly, he eased the covers off his legs, swinging around to a sitting position. Then he moved his weight onto his feet and tiptoed to the closed door, gripping at the carpet with his toes. He stopped after each step to listen, and his pulse pounded through his body.

Open the door? Or no? *Don't do it*, he heard the horror-movie audience whisper. *No, don't open the door, don't do it!*

He put his hand on the doorknob and soundlessly turned it, pulled the door toward him, and eased the knob back again. The hallway stretched out before him.

Two doors on the left, stairs to the right, and the reading nook that nobody used at the end. Moonlight came in through the reading nook's skylight, streaming over the gliding rocker and bookshelves to create a tangle of shadows on the floor.

Rith eased his way down the hall, the plush carpet giving beneath his bare feet. He stopped at the first door. That was Emma's room, filled with frills and dolls and a four-poster bed that she would sleep in when she was old enough. He put his ear up to the cool wood of the closed door to listen. Nothing. He stepped ahead to the bathroom and glanced in. The night light over the sink cast its glow around the toilet, and the shower stall was dark and still.

Rith crossed to the right side of the hallway and flattened himself tight against the wall, edging closer to the stairs. Then he took a deep breath and spun around the corner to stand full and center at the top—and he stumbled backwards, almost falling against the opposite wall.

They were the wrong stairs.

Instead of the wide, carpeted steps that went to the landing and then turned, a narrow wooden spiral staircase with a wooden railing wound its way down into darkness. No landing, just coils. He shook his head and blinked hard. He reached up and tugged on a pinch of hair. It hurt. He was definitely awake.

Rith moved forward a step and rose up on his toes, trying to see the bottom. He got down on his hands and knees and inched his hand across the carpet. Maybe there was a membrane between this and that. Maybe if he put his hand through, he'd be pulled in. He paused, his hand just on the edge of the carpet. Then he stretched.

He touched wood, ran the tip of his finger back and forth. It was smooth and cool. He scooted forward, the carpet rough against his bare knees as he moved. He put his palm on the step, rapped his knuckles on it. Plenty solid. He lay flat on his stomach and looked down.

A deep shadow flicked and dipped below, so fleeting that it might have been a trick of his eyes. Or maybe something moving down there. Rith sat back on his heels. What if he turned on a light? Not the overhead, just the one above the bathroom sink. That would open up the darkness a bit and he could see what was what.

He edged back toward the bathroom, keeping an eye on the stairs until he couldn't see them around the corner anymore. Then he reached in and flipped the switch, spilling light into the hallway. Two steps and he could see—carpet. All carpet. The wooden staircase was gone.

He quick-stepped to the top of the stairs. Carpet. All carpet.

Rith got down on his hands and knees at the top of the stairs, rubbing his hand across the second one down. Not wood. Maybe if he turned the light off again . . . ? He returned to the bathroom, reached in to flip the switch, and rushed back to the top of the stairs.

No good. Still carpet.

He cocked his head, listening. The refrigerator kicked on, rattling its way into a steady hum. The smoke detector's light glowed green from the ceiling above the landing. He sat on the top stair, digging his toes in the carpet of the step below. He had definitely heard a noise. Twice. The first time woke him up. The second time he'd been wide awake, eyes open. And just a minute or two ago, the stairs had been wood. Not carpet. Wood with a railing, spiraling down.

"You read too much," he said out loud.

His voice was hushed in the darkness, a little shaky.

"You think this is a book or something? You think it's a magic staircase and you'll go down and he's going to come walking in the front door?"

A wind blew through his voice, shaking it harder. Mom used to set a place for Dad at the table on Rith's birthdays. Way back when he was little. She thought he didn't remember but he did. Like Dad would be coming home, like maybe he'd sidestepped that head-on collision at the last minute and gone off on a little overseas adventure and would show up just in time for cake.

Then Walt came along and she'd stopped doing that, stopped talking about Dad completely. She wouldn't even answer Rith's questions, just gave him that line about the happy lives they had now. Ha.

Dead was dead was dead, Rith knew that. Wizards didn't show up at the door, dead dads didn't come back to life, and nobody found dragon eggs or went off on quests. They just went to school and did their homework and did what they had to until they were old enough they didn't have to anymore.

Rith went back to bed, turning for one last look over

his shoulder before closing his door behind him. He burrowed down under the sheet, wishing it was cooler so he
could pull a mountain of blankets over his head. Even
with the sheet it was too hot.

He kicked the sheet off and rolled onto his side. Then
he lifted his head off the pillow, listening. He'd heard
something—short and squeaky, like a baby or maybe a
mewly kitten—but it didn't come again. The house
hummed its way through the nighttime silence. Rith let
his head sink back onto the pillow and he fell asleep.

Rith dragged into school the next morning half-asleep. He came around a corner and almost ran into Toby.

"Hey Rith, there you are. I figured your locker had to be on this floor somewhere. Are you going to be at that class at church tomorrow night?"

"Why, are you coming?"

"Sure. I'm not doing the whole confirmation thing, I'm just monitoring. So I don't have to do the homework but I get to come to the classes."

"Get to?"

"Yeah. Even though my parents don't belong to the church."

The bell for homeroom rang and Rith shrugged out of his jacket.

"It's really boring," he said.

"Maybe we can kick it up some," said Toby. "Second bell, I gotta run. Later."

Rith shuffled through the morning, falling asleep during the video in fourth period history. He dozed on the school bus on the way home too, and was still half-asleep when he came in the front door. He kicked off his boots, hung up his jacket, and started up the stairs.

"Oh good, you're home," said Mom, coming from her bedroom. "I need you to go to the store with me."

"Right now?" said Rith, stopping on the landing.

"Yes, now. Come and help me get the kids ready. Emma's in the kitchen. Get her boots and jacket on while I get Ben."

Rith turned and went back down. At the foot of the wide carpeted stairs, he angled through the doorway to the kitchen, where he found Emma sitting on the tiled floor. She held up her blue boots, one in each hand.

"Elmo," she said. She dropped one boot and pointed to the grinning red Elmo on its side.

"Yup, that's Elmo," Rith agreed. "C'mon, get up on the chair here."

Mom's goo-gooing voice floated down the hall as she told Ben what an amazing little man he was. Rith lifted Emma up on the kitchen chair and knelt to jam the boots on her feet.

"Rit Rit Rit."

"Emma, do you have to say my name all dang day?"

"Rit," she insisted, patting the top of his head.

Once they got the kids strapped into their car seats and Rith settled into the front seat, he asked Mom, "Do you ever have dreams that are so real you can't tell they're dreams?"

"Can't say that I have. I usually don't remember

my dreams."

"I had this dream that was so real, I thought . . ."

Emma cut Rith off with a loud burble of toddler talk from the back seat.

"No, honey, we're not going to Jason's house today," said Mom.

"How can you tell what the chuck she's saying?" asked Rith.

"You know we don't like that expression," said Mom.

Rith rolled his eyes. Why always *we*? She used to think things all by herself.

"Rith, about this fishing trip Saturday," Mom said.

Rith's stomach clenched.

"I want you to try. Can't you just try?"

"Try what?"

"Try to have a good time."

Rith watched the suburban streets as they passed, the banks on the sidewalks cut back by snow blowers. Emma giggled and sputtered in back, and Ben hiccupped loudly.

"Please, Rith."

"What do you care if I have a good time or not? I have to go either way."

"Yes, you have to go. I'm just asking you to try. It's important to Walt."

Rith rolled his eyes at the passing cars, turned away so Mom couldn't see.

"You never know, you might like it if you let yourself. Besides, Tyler's going to be there. The two of you have fun together."

Rith regretted every time he had ever gotten along with Walt's nephew.

"You can make me go," he said, "but you can't make me want to."

They pulled into the parking lot of the grocery store and unloaded the kids. Rith carried Ben, while Mom pulled a chattering Emma along by the hand. They pulled out two carts and of course Emma had to ride in his, so he strapped her into the plastic baby seat and they trailed behind the head cart. The wheels rattled, staticky voices asked for price checks, and Mom hummed along to the Eagles music piping in. Rith was reaching for the laundry detergent that Mom pointed out when Emma hollered.

"Kitty!"

She lurched toward the cat food shelf, pointing at a picture of a gray cat on one of the boxes.

Rith grabbed her before she could upset the cart, and said, "Yup, kitty."

"Kitty!" she said, insistently.

"Right, kitty. And down here are the doggies."

Emma didn't care about the doggies. She reached for the cat food, yelling.

"Mom, Emma's freaking out," he called.

Mom, who was up ahead looking at fabric softeners, turned and looked back.

"What's wrong?" she asked.

"Kitty!" wailed Emma, amping up to a higher pitch.

"Emma, what's wrong, sweetie?" Mom walked back,

leaving Ben a few feet ahead in the other cart.

Emma sobbed, pointing at the cat food bag.

"Yes, that's a kitty," said Mom. "You're right. Good job. Now we have to go get some nice fabric softener."

"Kitty!" Emma screamed.

People turned to look at them, and now Ben let out a wail. Rith ducked away from Emma and slunk over to Ben, saying, "Shh, Ben, don't you start up too, okay?" One screaming baby in public was way more than enough.

Ben turned a wide-eyed gaze to Rith. Mom took over Emma's cart and steered it away from the cat food, past Rith and Ben.

"Emma kittttteeeeeeeeeeeee."

"No, honey, that isn't Emma's kitty. That is someone else's kitty. We don't have a kitty."

Rith followed, pushing Ben. When they turned the corner, Emma locked her bright blue eyes on Rith's face.

"Kitty," she said to him.

Like he was the only one who could possibly understand.

After dinner Rith went up to his room and pulled out his confirmation homework. He flipped the book open to the week's assignment. The whole page was about names. What is my name, what does my name mean, why was I given this name. Question after question jabbing right into the sore spot.

Rith went to the top of the stairs and hollered down.

"Mom! Hey Mom?"

"She's putting the kids to bed," Walt called from the living room. "What do you need?"

"Nothing."

Rith went back in his room and flopped on his bed, arms crossed over his chest. When he was little and Mom used to talk about his father, Rith was too dumb to ask important questions. So he knew that his dad's favorite color was purple and that he wanted to be a mountain climber and died in a car accident. But what was he really like? Was he funny? Strict? Tall? How old was he when his voice changed? And even though Mom said his dad named him, she never told him where the name came from or what it meant. Everyone else knew stuff like that.

Later, as he was brushing his teeth, Mom came up the stairs.

"Did you need something, Rith?"

Rith nodded and spit. He slurped some water from his hand and reached for the towel to wipe his face.

"You could use the cup, you know," said Mom. "That's what it's there for."

"Did we ever have a family Bible?" asked Rith, flipping off the light and walking past Mom to his bedroom.

"Why are you asking me that?"

Her voice came out sharp, harsh. Rith spun to look at her. She was still in the hallway.

"Confirmation homework," he said, pointing to his desk. "Did we?"

"Not the way they mean. Let's see what you're working on."

She stepped past him to look at the open book.

"See? Right there," he said. "It says, 'Do you have a family bible?'"

"No, we don't," said Mom.

"Well, what about this name stuff? I don't know how to answer it."

Mom folded her arms across her chest, looking down at the book.

"Your name is from a Greek word," she said. "Your dad picked it, I told you that."

"Greek? You never told me that before. Why a Greek word? Was Dad Greek? Did he speak Greek?"

He rapid-fired the questions at her and she took a step back, still looking toward the book.

"I don't know why Greek, Rith, that's just what he said. Maybe someone told him that, I don't know."

"Why don't you know? Didn't you ask him?"

"Maybe I did, I forget. He came up with the name and I liked it. Even when you were a baby it fit you perfectly. Now come on, it's late. Fill in those questions and get to bed."

"Why won't you tell me anything? It's an assignment." He jabbed his finger at the workbook. "I have to, remember?"

"The point of the assignment is baptism. And since you were old enough to remember yours, those other questions will be easy. The rest of the class can learn a lot from you."

Like he'd ever bring that horrible day up anywhere. He'd been in fifth grade, way too old, and he had to wear a tie. The whole thing had been humiliating.

"You're never going to tell me anything, are you?" he said.

Mom stepped back, her lips gone tight.

"You know the important things," she said. "Your dad loved you, that's what matters. If I knew what your name meant I'd tell you but I don't know. I went to the library and looked it up once but I couldn't find anything. Maybe your dad changed it or got the spelling wrong. Sometimes he got things mixed up."

"So are you saying he wasn't very smart? He goofed up my name? Or he made it up?"

"Don't put words in my mouth. I didn't say any of that. Now finish up and get to bed."

Rith watched her, waiting for a better answer. Her cheeks were bright red and she bit down on her lower lip.

"Rith, please."

He stared a moment more, then slammed into his chair.

"Okay, whatever," he said. "Who cares. It's not like we get graded on this stuff."

He scribbled short answers in each blank, so sloppy he could hardly even read them himself. He felt Mom relax behind him, felt her hands come down on his shoulders. They squeezed gently. She kissed the top of his head, said good night, and left the room.

He kept writing, his insides boiling and churning and flipping around. One minute it seemed like he was nothing but a problem, an ugly stinking problem, like she wished he would disappear out the window and never come back. Then came the shoulder squeeze and the kiss and just for a second it was like B.W. Back when she loved him best. But that was over.

Even though he'd felt tired doing the confirmation homework, Rith's eyes sprang wide open as soon as he turned off the light. He lay there staring at the darkness, running the conversation with Mom over and over in his head. What did it mean, sometimes he mixed things up? Things like what? Your kid's name, that was a big thing to mix up.

Rith opened the book on his nightstand, picking up where he'd left off. Questions continued to circle around in his head, but they faded as he read himself deeper into another world, far away from the bedroom and the homework and the sharp tone in Mom's voice. He read several chapters, then put the book down and crept over to his closed bedroom door, put his ear against the crack, and listened. Quiet. They'd gone to bed. He turned the knob and stepped into the hallway.

The hall was dark, no moon. He walked to the top of the stairs. Carpet, normal under his bare feet. Down the stairs to the landing, around the corner, into the kitchen. Nothing but the furnace running and the streetlights outside and the tile underfoot. Rith turned in place, looking all around. He stepped over to the sliding glass door and cupped his hands around his eyes to see the dark snow-covered patio. Everything outside was smooth and white, broken only by paw prints that came up to the door and went away again. Squirrel? Cat? Rith's breath fogged up the glass and he stepped back, wiping the foggy spot with his hand.

He closed his eyes, making a wish. When I open them, the stairs will be wooden. *Come on God, if there is a God. You're supposed to answer prayers, right? So do your job.*

He opened his eyes.

See. Nothing.

Wednesday night in the church basement, Rith took his usual seat in the soft rocking chair on the outer edge of the circle. Other kids came in and jammed onto couches and chairs all around the room while Christian rock played, words scrolling over a dramatic mountain scene on the screen in front.

"Rith," called Pastor Paul. "Rith Haley!"

Rith spun the chair, facing the doorway. Toby stood there next to the pastor.

"There's your pal," said Pastor Paul to Toby. "Rith, show him the ropes, will you? Make sure he doesn't get lost?"

Rith nodded, and Toby came over to sit in the straightback chair next to him.

"So. This is confirmation class, huh?"

"This is it," said Rith. "Hope you like Christian rock."

"Not your thing?" asked Toby.

"Not so much."

The song finished and Pastor Paul stepped up on the

platform and ran through the usual announcements about spaghetti dinner, youth mission trip, and whose turn it was to shovel the walks of the old people in the congregation. Then he launched into a talk about baptism. Rith closed his eyes and tuned out. *Blah blah blah.* Just like church, only the seats were more comfortable.

"Okay, small groups," called Pastor Paul. "Leaders, bring them back in forty minutes."

The room full of seventh, eighth, and ninth-graders churned into action as they sorted themselves into small groups by grade. Rith and Toby followed a gaggle of girls into one of the classrooms. They sat at the corner of the table, and the girls all stared at Toby like they'd never seen the species before.

"Name's Toby," he said, waving. "Hola, Elise, qué tal?"

"That's Toby Corbett. He's in my class," said Elise to the others.

Mrs. Hughes, the group leader, swept in before Elise could say anything else. She closed the door, locking her sweet thick perfume smell in the room.

"Toby Corbett," she said, spotting Toby. "So happy to have you. Welcome to our class. Do you know the others from school?"

"Just Elise and Rith," he said.

"Well this is Monica, and Natalie, and Tatum. And we're studying baptism right now, which is one of the two holy sacraments in the Lutheran church. Who would like to tell us the story of their baptism? Natalie?"

Natalie launched into a long story about her older

brother burping out loud in front of the church during her baptism, and the girls fell all over each other giggling. Mrs. Hughes smiled, nodding. She was one of those adults who smiled so she would look like she liked kids but anyone could see she didn't think it was funny. Although it sort of was.

Once the girls pulled themselves together they each told their story, going on and on like they usually did. On the best nights time ran out before they ever got to Rith. Mostly they forgot he was there.

"Toby? Would you like to tell us about your baptism?" asked Mrs. Hughes, leaning toward the boys.

"I didn't get baptized," said Toby. "My parents wanted to let me decide for myself."

"Does that mean if Toby dies, he'll go right to hell?" asked Natalie.

Mrs. Hughes acted like she hadn't heard. "Rith? Do you want to tell us your baptism story?"

"Um, Mrs. Hughes?" said Toby. "Excuse me, but will I?"

Silence beat around the room. Mrs. Hughes took a deep breath, opened her mouth, then closed it.

"Because that's what my dad said you guys would say," said Toby. "That you try to scare people into believing by threatening them with hell. And what do you know, the first night somebody did."

"Nobody is threatening anybody, Toby." Mrs. Hughes was quick with that answer. "I hope you'll stay long enough to learn more about our faith, and you'll see that Jesus doesn't make threats. Baptism is very important, yes. But we don't do it because we're afraid."

"Then why do you do it?"

Rith and the girls watched Toby and Mrs. Hughes like a tennis match.

"Because we love the Lord, that's why. It's time to go back to the big group now. Toby, if you have more questions you can ask Pastor Paul."

Mrs. Hughes and the girls filed out, and Toby and Rith were left alone in the room with the perfumey smell still crawling around the corners.

"Did your dad really say that?" asked Rith as they headed for the door.

"Yeah, my dad says all kinds of stuff," said Toby. "But I didn't expect him to be so right so fast. What happens next?"

"Wrap-up," said Rith. "Pastor Paul talks some more, prays, and cuts us loose."

"So should I really ask him?"

They rounded the corner back into the big room. Rith's usual chair was taken by a seventh grader, so Rith and Toby sat in folding chairs in back.

"Why not?" Rith shrugged. "I'd like to hear what he says."

As soon as Pastor Paul asked for questions, Toby's hand shot up.

"So since I'm not baptized, if I die on the way home will I go straight to hell?"

Pastor Paul cleared his throat a couple of times. Then, not looking at Toby but scanning across the room, he said, "Tell you what, let's not start with hell, let's start with heaven. The Bible says the one who believes and is baptized will be saved, and the one who does not believe will be condemned. So belief is the critical thing. If you love Jesus and believe that Jesus loves you, then you never have to worry about hell. Any other questions?"

"So baptism doesn't matter?" called out the boy who had taken Rith's seat.

"Of course baptism matters. Most of us were baptized when we were babies and we grow into our relationship with God. Some people learn about Jesus and get baptized later. It's not the order of events that matters so much as the faith itself."

"But what if so far I only like Jesus and I'm not sure I love him," said Toby. "And I get killed in a car accident and I'm not baptized. Then what?"

"These are complicated questions," said Pastor Paul. "In Romans, Paul says very clearly that it's not up to us to judge one another. That's God's job, and He can see what's in your heart. Faith is the critical thing, and you have a chance here to learn about Jesus's love and to step right into it. And as you do, there's no reason to put off being baptized."

"So if I—"

"Toby, why don't you come up and have a chat with me after the prayer. Maybe I can help you out with this. Let's pray."

He launched into a prayer, the usual stuff about guidance and blessings for youth, and then went into the Lord's Prayer.

"Wait for me?" Toby said to Rith after the amen.

"Sure, of course."

Rith settled back into the rocker and watched Toby and Pastor Paul talk. He couldn't hear, but it didn't look like trouble—Pastor Paul smiled, then laughed. After a few minutes Toby walked back to Rith, grinning.

"What'd he say?" asked Rith.

"He said it's like when you make a deal with someone. You don't have to sign a contract or shake hands, but those things make both of you more sure of the deal. He said baptism is like a sacred handshake. Usually your parents do it for you, but you can do it yourself."

"What was he laughing at?" asked Rith, slipping into his jacket.

"I asked him if the water is like when kids spit on their hands before they shake. For extra deal-sealing. And he laughed. Not fake-smile like that Mrs. Hughes, but a real laugh. Then he said, yeah, kinda like that, and he hoped I'd come back and get a deeper understanding."

The boys walked up the stairs and into the foyer.

"Do you think you will?"

"Probably," said Toby as he pushed the door open. "I've got a lot more questions about this whole thing."

"Good. It's definitely more fun with you here."

They walked out into the icy night. Stars were frozen across the sky and the snow glowed bluish white in the lights from the church.

"There's my dad," Toby said, pointing to a brown Volvo. "See you."

"Yeah, later," said Rith, turning to where Mom was parked in the big silver Escalade a few spaces back.

"Is that Toby from Sunday?" asked Mom.

"Yup."

"So you're not the only eighth-grade boy anymore?"

"Nope."

"Good. I'm glad."

For once, Rith and Mom were happy about the same thing.

The next day after lunch, Rith stopped by his locker to get his algebra book.

"Orithian Haley." The voice was deep in his ear and he spun around, whamming his funny bone on the edge of his locker door and dropping his books.

"Ah! Oh, geez Toby. Yow."

The jangling ran up and down his arm and out into his fingers.

"Hey, sorry dude. That was my Darth Vader voice, pretty good, huh?"

"Yeah, good," said Rith, spreading his fingers and then clenching his fist as the pain eased off. "Dang, that was my funny bone."

"Sorry." Toby bent over and picked up Rith's math book and binder. "Hey, you want to do something Saturday? Maybe meet at the mall for a movie or something?"

"Sure," said Rith. "I just gotta ask my . . . oh wait. I can't. I have to go ice fishing."

"Ice fishing? Is that fun?"

"No. It's anti-fun."

"Can you ditch it?"

"Maybe," said Rith. "I'll see."

After school, he took the garbage out without being told and picked a bunch of Emma's toys up off the kitchen floor and put them in her toy box. And when Ben's binky fell out of his mouth, Rith rinsed it at the kitchen sink before giving it back to him, checking to see if Mom noticed.

"So Mom," he said, after he'd given her a long full answer about how school was, even telling her about the poem they'd read in English. "You know Toby from church? He asked me to meet him at the mall Saturday."

"Oh, Rith."

"You know how you've been telling me I need to make friends, well now I am. If I say no he probably won't ask me again. Can I go? I promise I'll go ice fishing some other time and I won't even complain about it. Please?"

"I'm sorry, honey. Walt's been counting on this. I'm sure Toby will understand. Just tell him you can do it next weekend. Or he can come over here. We'd love to have him."

"Mom! How am I supposed to make friends if you won't let me?"

"Now Rith. You're not being fair. What about Walt?"

"Yeah, well life's not fair. Isn't that what you always say?"

"It's not up for discussion, Rith. Family comes first."

"*Your* family," he muttered under his breath as he stomped up the stairs, closing his bedroom door with as close to a slam as he could get without actually slamming.

He loaded up his CD player and cranked the volume. The music filled the room and rocked the walls. Rith paced around, letting the beat move into his body. He closed his eyes and jumped up and down, shaking the vibrations out his arms and into his fingers. The music and the angry words filled him, moved him, jerked him back and forth, and took him out of the room and out of the house.

He spun and almost tripped over Emma, stumbling to catch himself from falling on top of her.

"What are you doing in here?"

She smiled up at him, moving to the music. She danced like she was wading through mud, lifting one foot and then the other, her whole body rocking from side to side.

"How did you get in, anyway?" Rith demanded.

If Emma had figured out how to turn doorknobs, that was bad news. Up to this point a closed door had stopped her. She stomped with both feet, jumping up and down. Rith half-smiled. He'd never seen a baby dance to head-banger music. He danced around her and she followed him until her feet got away from her. She landed on her butt and laughed out loud.

"So you like this stuff?" said Rith. "Well, good for you."

He picked her up and tossed her on the bed, out of his way. The music worked its way back into his body and he danced hard, whipping his head back and forth and letting his brains rattle around in their cage. If only they'd play this at school dances instead of that stupid pop stuff all the girls liked. They should take lessons from Emma.

She bounced up and down on the bed, flapping her arms until the music ended. Rith stepped over to the CD player, skipping ahead a couple of songs. As the music started he picked her up and tossed her again. She burrowed into his pillows with her butt up in the air, then jumped back to her feet. They faced each other and Rith stomped and made faces. Emma's squealy giggle was almost as loud as the music. Then her eyes shifted off his face.

Rith turned and saw Mom smiling in the doorway with Ben in her arms. He stopped immediately and strode around the bed to turn down the volume. His face burned.

"I was just keeping Emma out of your hair for a minute," he said. "Can you get her out of here?"

"Sure. Come on, Emma. Come help Momma make dinner."

"Rit?"

"No, Rith's 'busy.' Come help Momma."

Rith lifted Emma off his bed and set her on her feet. Mom took the babies and left, closing the door behind her.

Friday night they all went to bed early, since Rith and Walt would be leaving before sunrise in the morning. Rith tossed and turned for a long time before he fell into a tangle of confusing, foggy dreams.

Then suddenly, he was awake. Eyes open, heart hammering away as if he'd just run up and down the stairs. He sat up, listening hard. The house was quiet. A half moon wavered behind the curtains, casting silver light across the room like a path to the door. He got up and pulled on sweatpants. Then he opened the door, letting the moonlight stretch into the hallway. The carpet, the walls, the closed doors, they pulled him out into the hall. He walked, looking toward the upper left corner of the reading nook. Would not let himself look at the stairs. Not until he got there. He stopped short, looking up and holding his breath. Then he did a sharp right-face and looked down.

Wood.

Rith reached a hand out to feel the air, searching for something that divided one world from the next. Nothing. Slowly, he began to descend. Step down, bring the back foot to meet the front one, pause, listen, look around. On the third step, he saw shadows shifting and moving in the darkness below. After the sixth step, the flickering light touched his feet and he squatted to see an unfamiliar room opened out below him.

Flames danced in a fireplace on the far side of the room. The hearth and chimney were made of smooth, round, gray stones of different sizes; a rough wooden mantel held a row of books. An oversize armchair spread its wings in front of the fire, and a narrow gray cat stood on the back of the chair, arched, looking directly up at Rith.

"Hi kitty," he said, softly, excited.

This was it! Whatever it was, this was it. He glanced back up, but could only see the undersides of the wooden stairs above him. They spiraled up, disappearing into the darkness above.

The cat made a meeping noise and Rith recognized it immediately as the one he'd heard a few nights earlier. He came down the rest of the stairs, turning his head to keep an eye on the cat as he spiraled around the center. Whatever kind of dream this was, it was going to be good. He could feel it.

Rith's feet reached the floor, also wood but not worn smooth like the stairs; it was rougher, uneven. The fireplace and chair were to his left, and to the right of the staircase was a square wooden table. Some unfinished cupboards lined the wall and a heavy, solid door stood on the other side. On one wall, a large, curtainless window opened out into the dark world. Rith stood at the bottom of the stairs, taking it all in. Then he stepped toward the cat, stretching out his hand.

"Be strong, and show yourself a man," said a quiet voice from the chair in front of him. "First Kings two two."

Rith stopped short, staring.

"Did you say that?" he whispered to the cat.

It pricked its ears forward. Rith took another hesitant step and saw white hair sticking up behind the cat. He rose on tiptoe. On the other side of the cat was the top of a head, mostly bald with white hairs straying.

"Hello?" Rith said, stepping around the chair.

The man sitting there didn't reply, didn't even look up from the book on his lap. He was small and old. Rumpled white hair shagged over the tips of his ears, tufting around the baldnesss on top. He wore a heavy green sweater and brown corduroy pants; a large book lay open on his lap. His eyes hid behind gold-rimmed glasses, and his hand, which rested on the book, was bent and bumpy and spotted with age.

"Who are you?" asked Rith.

"Come in, for you are a worthy man and bring good news," said the man in his soft, raspy voice. "First Kings one forty-two."

Rith wrapped his arms tight across his chest.

"Who are you?" he asked again.

The man continued to look down at the book as if he hadn't heard Rith. The cat had turned as Rith moved around him and now perched behind the man, the end of its tail twitching.

"Hey!" said Rith. "Can you hear me?" He shifted more in front of the man and pulled one hand out of his armpit to wave. "Can you see me here?"

The man looked up, not at Rith but at the fire. His eyes were old, pale in color, surrounded by bunches of wrinkles and magnified by the thickness of his glasses. He looked back down at the book, flipped some pages, and ran a crusty bent finger across the column of small print.

"A good name is better than precious ointment; and the day of death, than the day of birth. Ecclesiastes seven one."

"What does that—"

"Go up in peace to your house." The man cut him off. "First Samuel twenty-five thirty-five."

At that, the cat leapt from the chair and landed with a thump and a squeak at Rith's feet. Rith took a step back toward the heat of the fire. The cat moved ahead and to Rith's right, and he again stepped away.

"To your house," the old man repeated, louder but not looking up.

The cat made a low growling noise with another step toward Rith, its yellow eyes locked on him. Rith backed away, moving toward the stairs.

"Did I do something wrong?" he asked the cat.

The cat continued stepping toward him, herding him.

"First Samuel," repeated the old man. "Twenty-five thirty-five."

Rith backed all the way over to the wooden staircase and took one step up. The cat stalked to the foot of the stairs and stood there, its eyes following Rith as he backed up the spiral, step by step. What would he do if the carpet wasn't there at the top? When he'd gotten far enough up that he could no longer see the cat, he looked over his shoulder. Moonlight. He backed up a few more steps and looked again. Carpet, the reading nook, and the hallway. The house was right where it should be.

"What if I don't believe in you?" Rith called down. "Will that make you not be there?"

The sound from below was a clear cat meow, rising at the end like a question mark. Rith sat on the wood, a few steps down from the top. Shadows flickered below. He rubbed his hand across the smooth wood. This was the weirdest, realest dream he'd ever had.

"Go up in peace to your house," repeated the voice, raised enough to reach up the stairs. Rith scooted backward up the last few steps to the carpet at the top. He leaned forward. The stairs circled down into the darkness below. He stood and began to back down the hall toward his room, watching the wood to see if it would change. He took one more step, then another. He drew his head back just enough so he couldn't see the stairs, and then leapt forward.

Gone. Nothing but carpet. He went back to stand at the top of the stairs. The moon from the skylight showed carpet all the way. A straight shot to the landing. No spiral. He took a step down, stopped, waited. Then another.

He went all the way to the bottom and made the circle through the kitchen and living room. Everything was as quiet and normal as it could possibly be. He checked the patio for tracks and saw nothing but the trample of his own footprints from taking out the garbage. At the front door he flipped on the outdoor light. The bare porch and sidewalk had no clues, no signs of an old man or a cat.

Rith squeezed his eyes shut tight and shook his head hard. Then he opened them again, looking around the living room. He walked over to the entertainment center, running his palm over the cool TV screen. No fireplace, no warmth.

The green numbers on the DVD player told him it was 2:59. His alarm would be going off in about three hours. Rith returned to the second floor, rubbing the soles of his feet on each carpeted stair as he went. At the top he turned left and started toward his room, then suddenly jumped back toward the stairs.

Carpet.

He turned on the overhead light in his bedroom and looked at himself in the full-length mirror on the closet door. Dark eyes looked out from under the thick hair that dropped over his forehead. Pointy ears, sharp chin.

"You might be losing it," he said, pointing at himself. "For real."

His reflection tilted its head to the side and shrugged.

"Do you think this could get us out of ice fishing?" he asked himself.

He and his reflection shook their heads.

Rith got back in bed but he left the light on. No way he could sleep after all that. He picked up his book and read, but the whole time he was listening for a sound, any sound from the other side of the door.

Rith slammed his hand down on the top of the alarm clock, shutting off the squawking sound. Why was his light on? Jagged pieces of memory shuffled through his head. The wooden stairway, the cat. An old guy reading from—what—the Bible? Something about a good name. More than the words, Rith remembered the feeling of the dream. How he felt so wide awake, how he should have been freaked but wasn't.

"Rith? Are you awake?" Mom's voice came up the stairs.

"Yes," he called.

"Better get moving. Breakfast is almost ready."

Right. Ice fishing. A whole day with Walt. He looked around his room, his eyes stopping on the poster of Martin the Mouse Warrior with his sword and shield. Mouse warriors and wooden staircases—not real. Ice fishing—real.

"Rith!"

"I'm coming."

The morning was still pitch dark when Rith got in the Escalade with his iPod turned up and his Gameboy in hand. Walt threw the fishing gear in back, climbed into the driver's seat, and backed out of the drive. By the time they reached the freeway, the sky in the east had lightened to purple-gray and Rith was well into the fourteenth level. Walt reached over and pulled the Gameboy out of his hands.

"Hey!" said Rith.

"Here," said Walt, handing the Gameboy back to him. "Stow that for a while. And take those speakers out of your ears."

Rith put the Gameboy in his backpack and switched off his iPod, winding the cord around it.

Walt cleared his throat and Rith's stomach turned uncomfortably.

"We've got something important to talk about." Walt cleared his throat again. "I've been your stepfather for almost three years now."

Rith shifted in his seat, pulling the shoulder strap away from his neck.

"So I'd like to ask you to be my son, legally," said Walt.

Rith's chest squeezed in on itself. No air in. No air out.

"No disrespect to your dad. But you know, a boy needs a living father, especially when he's making the move to be a man. I'd like to adopt you. Make it official, get it on paper."

Rith kept his eyes turned out the window. The sky was

gradually lightening from black through shades of gray, like someone was turning up a dimmer light. The fields to his right stretched white and smooth to a dark rumple of trees on the far side.

"It's a big step, changing your name. I'd like you to have mine. It'd be good for all of us, bring us closer together. Less confusing for Emma and Ben—for every-one—if we all have the same name. I count on you as their big brother, you know."

Right. Precious babies. Not enough that they have their real Daddy Daddy Daddy, they need everything else per-fect too.

"Your mom and I think it's time we made this move, step into being a solid family. Sound right to you?"

They couldn't make him. Could not make him change his name. Could they? The highway lines passed *da-dump da-dump* beneath the tires. Walt cleared his throat again.

"All right, great. Jack at work gave me the name of his lawyer, I can make a call and get this rolling."

Da-dump da-dump da-dump. Same as all their serious talks; Walt talked and Rith didn't. No point. If he said anything, Walt would just tell him he was wrong, so why bother? Walt wanted him to say, Oh goody, I was hoping you'd adopt me. Anything else wouldn't even register.

Walt finally quit waiting for Rith to cheer and clap his hands. He switched on talk radio. Rith put his earbuds back in and turned the music up as high as it would go. Daylight had arrived but the sun still lurked beneath the horizon, casting a dull yellow wash on the eastern sky.

The long trip ended with a slow drive across the lake. They pulled up to the ice-fishing shack that Walt shared with his brother, Don. Don's truck was already there, and Don and Tyler popped their heads out. Walt was hardly out of the Escalade when his nephew Tyler crashed into him at full speed and almost brought him down. Tyler was a head taller than Rith and maybe thirty pounds heavier. Walt absorbed the blow and took Tyler down to the ice, rubbing snow in his laughing face.

"Can't bring the old man down yet, can you, Ty?"

Rith got out and shut the door. The low-hanging sun hit him full in the eyes, making him squint and turn in the other direction. Ty jumped up, brushing off the snow, and punched Rith in the arm.

"Hey Rith-man."

"Hey," said Rith, resisting the urge to rub his arm. He never felt smaller than he did around Ty.

"You boys get our stuff out of the back, there. Let's get down to some fishing. You got breakfast ready for us, little brother?" asked Walt.

"Just about," said Don. "Come on in and chow down."

The ice-fishing shack was new. It was a big one with paneled walls, a table, benches, and even a little sleeping loft overhead. The heater was going, and Don and Ty had already pulled up the floor panels, drilled the holes, and dropped four lines.

Don fried up some burgers on the hot plate and passed the jug of milk for everyone to drink out of. He slapped buns onto paper plates and passed them around. Rith ate quietly while the other three talked sports. Ty, who had been Mr. Man since his eighth-grade football team went undefeated, told about his winter conditioning program and how he was probably going to play varsity his freshman year.

"How about you, Rith? asked Don. "Any ideas about a sport you want to play in high school?"

Rith shrugged. "I dunno. See if there's rock climbing, I guess."

"Rock climbing? What kind of a sport is that? Is that a sport now?" asked Walt.

Rith shrugged again. "I dunno. Probably not."

"Hey, it's great conditioning, though," said Ty. "I tried it once on a climbing wall, and it's a lot harder than it looks. Maybe we can go sometime, Rith."

"Maybe," said Rith.

Rith pulled out his Gameboy and settled back into the corner of the bench farthest away from the rods. The other three sat around the holes, talking about football and pulling up the occasional fish.

"Hey Rith, wanna play some catch?" Ty asked after a while, standing and stretching. "Nothing's biting much, anyway."

"No, I'm going to go take a walk," said Rith, setting down the Gameboy and reaching for his jacket.

The only thing worse than being crammed in the ice-fishing shack was playing football with the Terrific Ty. He closed the door of the shack behind him and took a deep breath. Cold air rushed to the bottom of his lungs. Rith walked along a snowmobile track past the cars and trucks and SUVs, past all of the shanties, out to where the frozen lake spread itself far and wide without a sign of life. The sky was a bowl of bright clear blue and the sun shone yellow, like it had been drawn with sharp new crayons.

The wind was cold in his face, refreshing after the close dim air in the shack. He couldn't think inside, but out here the memory of the night came back full and clear. The warmth of the fireplace, the intensity of the cat's yellow-eyed stare. The old man's raspy voice. Rith balled his fists together inside of his gloves, tucking the thumbs in the middle to get them warm. He crunched along the icy track, nylon wind pants swishing.

The farther he got from the shacks and cars, the more Rith's chest loosened up. He took in full breaths, letting the fresh cold slice all the way in. The snowmobile track curved left and Rith stepped off into the windswept powder, his boots sinking with each step. On this end of the lake, the expanse of white was unbroken. It stretched out in all directions, rainbow bits of light sparkling in the sun.

Rith began to shuffle through the snow. He walked in a big circle, making a round, fat O. To the right of that, he walked a short line up, a two-step arc to the right, and back down. Another short line, then he jumped out to make the dot on the i. More forward and back for the t, h, and another i. Around and back for the a, then the curved top of an n.

Rith came back to the baseline and started the capital *H*. Double thick, block letters. Stomp stomp stomp, then jump over to start the next letter. He printed HALEY loud and hard in the snow. *Orithian HALEY*. He started going over the HALEY again, and by the time he caught the movement of Ty's bright blue jacket in the corner of his eye, it was too late to cover what he'd been doing.

"Haley, huh," said Ty, walking slowly along the baseline to read.

Rith, standing in the fork of the *Y*, nodded. "That's right. Haley."

"Uncle Walt told us about the adoption thing. You could do a lot worse than him for a dad."

Rith looked at Ty's red cheeks and blue eyes. He looked like Emma and Ben.

"I have a dad," said Rith. "And I have a name."

"Why do you gotta be like that, Rith? You don't even remember your real dad. Why don't you just go with it?"

Rith finished the *Y*. Then he came back down to the baseline and stomped out a heavy underline beneath HALEY.

"Hey, suit yourself," said Ty. "What do I care?"

Rith didn't look up until he finished going all the way over HALEY again. By that time, Tyler had disappeared in the clutter of shanties and vehicles littering the ice. Rith looked up and drew the sharp cold air into his chest.

"Orithian Haley," he said to the ever-deep blue of the sky. "My name is Orithian Haley."

Toby was just getting out of the brown Volvo when they drove into the church parking lot the next morning.

"Hey! Toby!" called Rith, bouncing out of the SUV while Mom and Walt detached the babies from their car seats.

"Hey dude," said Toby. "You survived the ice fishing."

"Barely. Way too much Walt time."

"You got coat-hanger duty again today?" Toby asked as they walked up the stairs.

"Yup, last time. Some other family does it next month."

The door opened behind them as Mom and Walt and the kids came in. Once they got the babies unbundled and coats hung, they stationed themselves at the doorway for greeting.

"So do you hate him or what?" whispered Toby, nodding toward Walt.

"He wants me to change my name," said Rith out of the corner of his mouth.

"Change your name? To what, Herman? Clarence?"

"No, not Orithian. The Haley part. He wants to adopt me and change my name to his."

The door opened and the first wave of people came in. The boys took coats, passing close by each other to exchange words in low voices.

"And lose Haley? What's his last name?"

"Kurth," said Rith, putting every bad feeling he had about Walt into the word.

He took another coat and hung it up. Toby stepped over close to whisper in his ear.

"Rithhhhhh Kurthhhhhhh? Whoa. Not so good."

"That's what I think."

They stopped talking as the coats surrounded them on all sides. Once the crowd thinned out and Mom and Walt took the babies to the nursery, Toby turned to Rith again.

"Do you like him at all?" Toby asked. "Apart from the name?"

Rith shook his head.

"So what did you say?"

"Doesn't matter what I say. Walt's just going ahead like it's all decided. That's what he's like. Walt wants it, *bang*, everyone has to do it."

"But they can't make you do that, can they? I mean if you were little they could, but don't you have some kind of say in it?"

Mom and Walt came back up, and the four of them went into church together. It wasn't until well into the sermon that Toby ripped a corner of paper from the bulletin and borrowed Rith's pen. He printed in tiny letters and passed the note to Rith.

Keep the comet!

Rith folded the scrap of paper and put it in his pocket. Add one real-world, wide-awake vote for Haley.

Over the next few days, Rith wondered how the adoption thing worked. Didn't he have to talk to a judge or something? Or did the adults just do a bunch of stuff and then wham blam, his name was Kurth? Walt had said something about a lawyer and getting paperwork going, so it would have to take a while, and maybe by then he could figure a way to get out of it.

He wished he had said something to Walt, something like, *Let me think about it* or *Can we wait for my next birthday* or *How about in eight million years . . .* but it was too late now. Walt had probably already paid a lawyer. If Rith told Mom he didn't want to, she'd probably cry. And Walt would get mad and say stuff about growing up and facing reality. If Haley was precious ointment, then Kurth was the greasy glop at the bottom of the sink when you finish doing the dishes.

Rith set his alarm Sunday night for 2:45 A.M., on the off chance that the old guy and the cat weren't a dream. When the alarm went off, he checked the carpeted stairs, the living room, and the kitchen. He looked at his reflection in the patio door and told himself to quit being a whack job and go back to sleep.

The next night at 2:47 he awoke not to the alarm but to

the feeling, pulling him out of a sound sleep. Out of bed and down the hall. He stared at the top wooden stair and blinked a few times. He rubbed his hands hard over his face to wipe the sleepiness away, then hurried down the spiral with a huge burst of happiness spreading through his chest.

"You came back," said Rith, rounding the chair. He sat on the stone hearth, facing the old man. The stones beneath him were warm and the fire was hot on his bare back. He shifted to the side, out of the direct heat.

"Can you read me that thing about the name again?" said Rith. "And tell me where it is, so I can . . ." He stopped, not wanting to offend the guy by saying he wanted proof of his existence.

"Give instruction to a wise man and he will be still wiser; teach a righteous man and he will increase in learning. Proverbs nine nine," the man read, nodding. Then he paged ahead and read, "A good name is better than precious ointment; and the day of death, than the day of birth. Ecclesiastes seven one."

"Ecclesi-whatsis seven one," Rith repeated, printing it into his memory. "Better than. Not like precious ointment, better than. So what are you? You're not a dream, right? Because I'm awake."

The cat came gliding around the chair and sat in front of Rith, curling its tail around itself and fixing its eyes on him.

"Hi kitty," he said, reaching out.

The cat moved its head back, glaring at Rith's outstretched hand.

"Right," Rith said, pulling it back. "Sorry. I was just try-ing to be friendly."

The cat blinked. Friendly from a distance.

"So that name thing," said Rith. "I've got a problem with that. It's all I have from my dad and they want me to change it."

The Bible Man flipped pages, then spoke again. "The father of the righteous will greatly rejoice; he who begets a wise son will be glad in him. Proverbs twenty-three twenty-four."

Rith had always wondered if his dad would like him. To be glad in him—he couldn't even imagine that.

"My dad never even knew me," he said.

The cat stretched out and started to purr, and Bible Man raised his head from the Bible to look into the fire. The cat continued to gaze at Rith. It had white whiskers and one white eyebrow hair sticking straight up. The purring was smooth and warm, inviting Rith to say more.

"And if he did, he might not like me. I hurt my mom all the time, even when I don't mean to. That's what's so bad about this adoption thing—I can't figure how to get out of it without making her get upset. I hate it when she cries. Makes me feel like . . . I don't know. If my dad was only here, everything would be different."

The light from the fire reflected in Bible Man's glasses so Rith couldn't see his eyes, but he gave the slightest nod of the head, permission to continue. Words Rith hadn't ever spoken aloud started to chug up from inside of him.

"I wish I knew him. I bet he was a great guy. I know he liked purple," Rith ticked the things off on his fingers, "and he worked construction and he wanted to climb mountains. That's it. Do you know I've never even seen a picture of him, not once? Mom said they didn't have a camera. That's kinda hard to believe. Seems like there would be school pictures or something. She just clams up whenever I ask. She told me last week that he got things mixed up sometimes, whatever that means."

Rith stood and walked over to the window. He had thought so many times about the things he wished he knew. It made him mad at the little boy who didn't know enough to ask. Did Dad hate sports? Was he good at math? The window was a dark mirror, reflecting Rith's face and the firelight behind. He turned back to Bible Man and the cat. The cat's eyes continued to follow him, but Bible Man still gazed quietly ahead, watching the fire.

"He died in a car accident in Florida. I don't even know what he was doing in Florida."

Rith never talked this much. Never. Not to anyone.

"If it wasn't for Walt I'd know. Mom used to talk about my dad sometimes, but once Walt showed up, she quit. He probably made her stop it."

The cat made a soft little squeak sound, and Rith came back over to sit on the hearth again. He leaned forward and talked to the cat.

"Mom used to put a plate on the table for him on my

birthdays and pretend he was there. I remember that. Then Walt shows up and *wham*, Kyle Haley is gone. Poof. Except for one little problem." Rith thumped his chest with his palm. "Me."

The cat looked back at him, the end of its tail waving slightly.

"And here's the thing I really don't understand—how could she marry Walt?"

Rith turned and gazed into the fire.

"Sometimes she's still like she used to be. When it's just her and me. But that hardly ever happens, especially since Ben got born."

He shook his head, turning back to the cat.

"How can she think I'd want to be Walt's son? He's too dense to even figure out that I hate him."

Bible Man jerked, like Rith had just woken him. He flipped some pages and read.

"He who conceals hatred has lying lips, and he who utters slander is a fool. Proverbs ten eighteen."

Rith felt slapped.

"Hey, I thought you were on my side!"

The cat stood, arching its back and looking sideways like a Halloween cat, and Bible Man flipped through pages. He stopped, studied the page closely, and read.

"Where there is no guidance, a people falls; but in an abundance of counselors there is safety. Proverbs eleven fourteen."

Then, for the first time, Bible Man took off his glasses and looked directly at Rith. The light blue watery eyes looked all the way into him like they were scouring through his brain, reading everything there. Rith shivered despite the heat of the fire burning behind him. He felt a pressure in the back of his throat and swallowed it down. That was one thing he had learned from Walt; he could make himself not cry. He had not cried in almost two years, not once.

Rith shifted, looking into the fire. The flames licked up around a big log, and a single splinter stuck out, glowing. The fire hissed softly but Bible Man and the cat stayed silent, waiting. When Rith finally dared to glance up, Bible Man was still looking at him, nodding slowly, and the warmth of the fire was in those pale eyes. The cat slowly stretched itself out again, long and lanky on the carpet, and resumed purring.

Back when Rith was little, Mom used to help him with his homework in the tiny kitchen of their old house. When he'd get confused, she'd look right at him and put her palm on his cheek, and he couldn't hide anything from her. Bible Man's gaze felt like that warm hand.

"So what am I supposed to do?" Rith asked, trying to keep his voice from shaking. "Mom knows I don't like him, I don't lie about it. And there's no point saying it to him, he just does whatever he wants anyway."

"Like a dog that returns to his vomit is a fool that repeats his folly," said Bible Man, his voice soft.

"Dog vomit?" Rith half-snorted the words, his shivering emotions coming out in a nervous laugh. "In the Bible?"

Bible Man put his glasses back on and turned some pages.

65

"Proverbs twenty-six eleven," he said, looking down.

"All right, Proverbs. But what's that supposed to mean? It's not like I have a choice about anything. Mom's on his side no matter what. Like that time she told me I'd better not mess this thing up for her."

The cat leapt onto the hearth and curled next to Rith's leg, purring loudly. Inviting him to pet it. Rith tentatively reached out and the cat leaned its head into his hand. Its fur was so soft and warm, it eased some of Rith's nerves, helped him to stop shaking. He ran his hand along the curve of its back.

"Can you say it again?"

"Like a dog that returns to his vomit is a fool that repeats his folly." Bible Man said the words slowly, patiently, one at a time. "Proverbs twenty-six eleven."

"I still don't get it." Rith shook his head. "Are you saying I'm repeating some folly? That means a mistake, right? But what?"

"He who speaks the truth gives honest evidence," said Bible Man. "Proverbs twelve seventeen."

Then he closed the large black Bible, took off his glasses, and dropped his chin to his chest. The cat purred on beneath Rith's hand.

"Hey, wait. Don't go to sleep. Aren't you going to tell me what this stuff means?"

Bible Man didn't move. His eyes stayed closed.

"Can't you just talk? Do you have to read everything?"

Rith glanced down at the cat. Its slitted eyes showed a thin line of reflection from the firelight as the purring continued to vibrate through Rith's hand.

"Is that it?" he asked the cat.

The cat uncurled and leapt from the hearth to the floor. It stood directly in front of Rith, looking at him. Then it looked over at the stairs. Three times, it did this.

"Is that dream-kitty language for go up to your house?"

The cat made a low throaty sound, almost a growl. Another shiver passed through Rith as he stood. The cat stalked around behind him, following him closely to the stairs.

"You're going to come back though, right?" Rith said as he began to spiral up. "Tomorrow night, maybe?"

The cat didn't answer.

Tuesday morning Rith woke to a cool hand on his forehead.

"Are you all right?" Mom asked. "You don't seem to have a fever."

He shifted his eyes around the room. How could it all look so normal, so everyday after all that happened in the night?

"This is the third time I've called you," Mom said, picking up the book from the floor beside Rith's bed. "Were you up late reading?"

"Yeah, I guess so."

She shook her head.

"You can't do that, Rith. If you won't get to sleep on time we're going to have to start checking on you."

We again. Why bring Walt into it?

"Okay, okay, I'm up," he said.

"Hurry now. Less than half an hour to bus time."

She left the bedroom door open. Rith got up, closed it, and stretched his mind back to the fire lit room. Ecclesi-

something. Seven one. He pulled his Bible off the shelf and looked in the front for it—there it was, Ecclesiastes. He turned to it, his fingers slipping on the thin pages. *It's not going to be there, it's just a dream, made up . . .* and there it was, right after the big bold seven. *A good name is better than precious ointment.*

"It's really there," he said out loud, and read it again.

He ran his fingers over the words, drinking them in through his fingertips.

"No kidding. It's really, really there."

"Rith! Breakfast, come on."

He got dressed and rushed to eat and catch the bus. On the way to school he pulled out a notebook and wrote down everything he could remember. Dog vomit, rejoicing father. Lying lips. Something about counselors. And the last thing about speaking truth. He remembered that one, remembered Bible Man's watery eyes and the raspy voice. *He who speaks the truth gives honest evidence.*

That night at dinner, Walt passed Rith a plate and said, "Things are moving along, Rith. I met with the lawyer today at lunch to go over the paperwork." He turned to Emma. "What do you think about that, baby? Should we have a big-brother party?"

Rith almost gasped out loud. He didn't know it was going to happen that fast—it had only been a few days. He looked down, his eyes narrowed. He hadn't agreed to anything. *He who speaks the truth* ran through his mind and he took a deep breath, feeling Bible Man's eyes on him. What if he did it? What if he really . . .

He cleared his throat.

"I, uh, I . . ."

Everyone turned to look at him, even Baby Ben. Emma stopped humming and considered him seriously, big blue eyes under blonde curls. Rith's face burned. If he were a Kurth he'd be bright flaming red the way Walt got when he was mad. But Rith was a Haley and a good name was better than precious ointment.

"About the, the adoption thing. I . . ."

Rith looked down at his plate and said it in a rush.

"I like my name. Haley. It's my dad's name and I like it."

There. It was out. Honest evidence.

Ben dropped his bottle on the floor and started to whimper. Rith snuck a quick glance at Mom, expecting that disappointed look she got every time he ducked out of doing something with Walt. It wasn't there. She looked surprised, and something else. Something he couldn't quite read. He looked down again, confused. Ben fussed louder but for once, everyone ignored him.

Walt cleared his throat, and Rith flinched.

"You've thought about this," Walt said.

Rith darted his eyes up. Walt's face and neck were red, but he didn't look mad.

"I want to keep my name like it is."

His voice came out strong. Not edgy, just clear. Walt nodded slowly. Ben squawked louder, and Mom picked up the bottle and plugged it in his mouth.

"I can see that," said Walt.

"How about if we do the adoption without changing your name?" asked Mom.

Rith hadn't thought about that. He looked at the cream-colored cloth napkin he'd been wringing and twisting. How could he say no to that? He had to give a reason.

"I don't know. I mean, like you said, give it some thought. Seems like I should, like you said. Do that. Can I think about it?"

Mom and Walt exchanged a glance, and secret messages passed back and forth between their eyes.

"Fair enough," said Walt, nodding. "Fair enough."

Rith quietly let out the breath he'd been holding.

"All done," said Emma, tugging at her bib.

Mom turned to help Emma take her bib off and to pull Ben out of the high chair. Rith quickly finished the food on his plate and excused himself. Walking up the wide, carpeted stairs, he had a new feeling in his chest. It worked. He spoke the truth, and he got to keep his precious ointment name.

That night something woke him and he was out of bed before he even got his eyes open. He stepped into the hallway and listened. It wasn't a cat. It was Walt. Rith tiptoed down to the landing and sat on the soft carpet there.

"It's not right, I'm telling you."

Mom's reply was softer, and her words were indistinguishable.

"You saw the kid at dinner. He's not a little boy any-more, Jane. It's time he faced reality, all of it. Hell, he doesn't even know what reality is. He walks around all the time in a made-up story, it's no wonder he doesn't do anything like a real boy. No sports, no outdoors, no friends, just computer games and books and that damn iPod."

More murmuring. Rith caught *too soon* and *won't have you something something.*

"How's he supposed to decide anything if he only has half the picture? For a nickel I'd go wake him up and tell him right now."

"Don't you dare, Walt. I mean it." Rith's eyes widened. He'd never heard Mom talk to Walt like that.

"Well, you know I won't. But I think you're dead wrong. You're going to have to deal with this or it'll come back and bite you in the butt."

Murmur murmur from Mom, and then the door between the kitchen and the living room swung open. Rith froze, making himself small on the landing. The things Walt had said twisted and roiled inside of him.

Half the picture about what? What was that supposed to mean, not like a real boy? Walt should mind his own goddang business. But . . . he was right about Rith not being a little kid anymore. Not that Rith cared what Walt thought, but he was right. And what was going to bite Mom in the butt?

The light went off in the kitchen and Mom swung through the door and crossed the living room. Rith moved his hand across the carpet he was sitting on, feeling its roughness. No way Bible Man would come tonight, not with all that going on.

The week dragged. Bible Man didn't come and the house was thick with tension. Walt left early and worked late, and Mom acted like a robot. Rith spent most of his time in his room.

The high point of the week was confirmation class, even though it wasn't quite as good as the week before. It helped just having Toby there—someone to sit next to and talk to during the break.

"You gotta go ice fishing again this week?" asked Toby after class as they were putting their jackets on.

"Nope. Thank God for that."

Rith and Toby tromped up the stairs with the rest of the crowd. The door opened and shut and kids ran out, skidding on the slippery sidewalk. Rith stepped up to the window, cupping his hands to see the street.

"So you want to come to my house?" Toby asked. "Dad said if your mom brings you Saturday around noon we can go to the mall and you can stay overnight. They'll bring you to church Sunday morning. Hey, is my dad out there yet?"

"Yeah, he's parked up near the corner. Let me ask, I think my mom'll let me."

"Cool. Let me know, okay?"

"Okay," said Rith, zipping his jacket. "Here goes."

They blasted out the doors and the wind stung Rith's

face. He skidded over to the Escalade and opened the door. Mom had both babies strapped in, meaning Walt hadn't come home from work yet. Ben was asleep, and Emma was banging a plastic hammer on the window and making blurbedy noises.

"So Mom," said Rith as he fastened his seat belt. "Can I go to Toby's this Saturday? His dad will bring me to church on Sunday."

"Sure hon, that's fine," she said.

She pulled out and drove home without a single question about confirmation class or anything else. The radio played softly as they drove past the warm-lit houses. When they pulled into the garage, Rith got the sleeping Ben out of his car seat while Mom turned Emma loose. Rith went upstairs and called Toby with the good news while Mom put the babies to bed.

When he went down to the kitchen later for a glass of milk, the house was dark. He flipped on the light as he came into the kitchen, and he and Mom both jumped.

"You scared me," he said. "Why are you sitting in the dark?"

Mom moved her hands across her face, rubbing her eyes and pushing her hair back.

"Daydreaming, I guess."

"It's night."

She half smiled and shook her head. "Night, then."

"Walt still not home?"

"He's working late again. What are you doing down here? Don't tell me Emma snuck up to your room again.

I thought she was down for the night."

"No," said Rith. "I'm just getting a glass of milk. Mom, is everything okay?"

She didn't really close her eyes—it was just a long blink. Long enough to make Rith's stomach do a half-skip sidestep. Something really was wrong.

"Are you after a snack?" she asked. "I think there's some cookies left in the cookie jar."

"No, just milk."

He didn't move, though. He stood watching her and she twitched—the same way he wiggled under her eyes when he tried to lie to her. She got up and went to the cupboard, getting out a glass.

"I can do that, Mom."

"I know you can, Rith," she said, handing it to him.

He turned and opened the refrigerator. She hugged him from behind, planting a kiss on top of his head. For just a minute he relaxed and let her hold him close. Like she used to.

"Mama!" Emma's voice came from the nursery. "Mama!"

Mom held Rith for another moment, long enough for him to think maybe, this one time, she'd rather be his mom. Just his.

Toby's dad came around from the backyard in a puffy down jacket as they pulled into the Corbetts' drive on Saturday. Mom rolled down her window and said hello while Rith grabbed his backpack and got out.

"Orithian Haley," Toby's dad said as Mom backed out with a wave and a toot. "So glad you could make it. You can call me Eric."

"Dad," Toby called, opening the front door. "Don't make him stand out there talking in the cold. Come on in, Rith."

"After you," said Eric, and they went inside.

"Come on upstairs, you can dump your stuff in my room," said Toby. "Then Dad'll take us to the mall."

"Right," said Eric, taking off his jacket. "Chauffeur at your service. Don't think you have to actually converse with me or anything."

"Dad!" said Toby. "Sheesh. We'll talk to you at dinner, all right?"

"I'll put it my calendar," he said, pretending to write on his hand as he walked away. "Dinner tonight, converse with son."

Rith followed Toby upstairs to the small bedroom at the end of the hall. When Toby opened the door, the first thing Rith saw was a dragon just above eye level, ready to fly through the doorway.

"Whoa!" said Rith, stepping in and looking around. "Wow, that's a lot of dragons!"

"Yeah, over the top, huh? Sometimes I think it's time to grow up and at least get new wallpaper, but it's gonna break my dad's heart. This one's his favorite. We built it last year."

Toby knelt on the bed and reached up, spinning a dragon with a four-foot wingspan.

"There's so many of them," said Rith, stepping over to the shelves and picking up a wooden dragon carving.

"I know. It's that thing where once you're into dragons, everyone gives you more dragons. Let's get the chauffeur and go."

Rith and Toby rode in the back seat to the mall, each plugged into one of Rith's iPod earbuds. Toby's dad kept turning up his classic rock radio station to bug them, but it didn't work. The collision of music made for a disjointed mix that Rith actually liked. Eric dropped them off at the south entrance and they bumped around through the crowds, in and out of stores.

"Did you ever do the climbing wall here?" asked Rith. "In the park?"

"No, I didn't even know there was one," said Toby.

"It's just a small one," said Rith. "But there's a twenty-dollar bill at the top of the advanced climb, and if you reach it, you get to keep it. Want to try?"

They found the wall in the center of the amusement park and each paid for two tries. Rith took the intermediate wall for a warm-up and Toby tried the beginner section. Toby fell off pretty quickly, but Rith made it to the top.

"You're good," said Toby, stepping out of his harness. "How'd you get so good?"

"I think it's in the genes," said Rith, shifting to the advanced wall. "My dad was into climbing, plus we had this huge rock by my house when I was little. I climbed on it all the time."

"Well come on," said Toby. "Let's see you get the twenty."

Rith only made it about halfway before his foot slipped while he was making a wide reach for the next stone.

"Take my other turn," said Toby as Rith started to unbuckle the harness. "It's a waste on me, and you might actually get the cash."

The second time Rith made it past the wide reach and didn't fall until the last stretch.

"Nice," said Toby. "I wonder if anyone ever makes it?"

"Someday I'm going to," said Rith. "If my arm was just a couple of inches longer, I think I could do it."

The mall with Toby was totally different than dragging around behind Mom and the babies. They ate their way through the food court, ending with ice cream. The theater was on the opposite side of the circular mall and Toby suggested a race. They took off in opposite directions and Rith ducked and dodged through the crowds, sprinting up the escalator to arrive about thirty seconds ahead of Toby. Panting and laughing, they bought their tickets and slid into the back row just as the previews started.

After the movie, the boys leaned against the wall in the mall entryway to wait for Eric.

"So why'd you start coming to church?" asked Rith. "I never would go if I didn't have to."

A group of high school kids came in the door with a blast of cold air. Once they'd passed, Toby said, "My mom's cousin died in December and we went to the funeral in Chicago. There was this lady pastor, and the way she talked, I dunno. Made me feel like I was missing something."

Rith glanced over. Toby was looking down at his foot and scuffing at a rough spot on the dirty carpet.

"How'd she talk?"

"Like she'd found this great thing and wanted to give you some. My dad says some people are really good speakers and you have to take that into account, but still. Lots of people believe this stuff, so maybe there's something to it."

"Why'd you pick our church?"

The Volvo pulled up to the curb and honked.

"It's close to home," said Toby, zipping up his jacket.

"And my mom's friend's sister goes there."

They ran out through the cold wind and slid into the backseat of the Volvo.

Later at dinner, Rith sat at the small round table in the Corbetts' kitchen. Toby's mom, Liz, dished up dark blue plates full of spaghetti and topped it off with a chunky red sauce. Eric poured tall glasses of milk and passed around a basket of hot rolls.

"How was the movie, boys?" asked Liz as they started eating.

"A dog," said Toby. "But not a bad dog. Maybe an Irish Setter. Not a Chihuahua."

"So Rith, this church you go to," said Eric. "Toby won't tell us much. How do you like it?"

"Eric," said Liz in a warning voice.

"Listen, Rith," said Eric. "If I offend you, just tell me you'd rather not discuss it, okay? But I'm curious. Do you like church?"

Rith glanced over at Toby, who shrugged. He decided to give the truth-speaking thing another try.

"Not so much. I'm actually a heathen. I don't believe."

Eric laughed out loud, and Toby yelled, "Hey, I didn't know that."

"What do your parents think about that?" asked Liz.

"Parent." Rith twirled spaghetti on his fork. "My dad's dead. And my mom and Walt don't know."

Eric sat back in his chair and grinned.

"Just like I said," he said, running his hand over his freckled bald head.

"No, Dad," said Toby. "What you said was, they were going to brainwash me. Here's Rith who goes every week and his brain seems fine, so what are you worried about?"

"He's got a point on you there," said Liz.

"Okay, point taken," said Eric. "Rith, what do you think would happen if you told them you don't believe in God? Or if you said that in confirmation class?"

"Dad, come on," said Toby. "He came over to hang out with me, not so you could prove there's no God and church is evil."

"Not fair!" yelled Eric. "That's not what I'm trying to prove at all. I mean, I actually do believe in a higher power, you know that."

"Right," said Toby. "The Force."

"Like in *Star Wars*?" asked Rith.

"Exactly," said Eric. "The forces of good. I believe in those. And like the song says, Jesus is just all right with me. Do you know that one? I could sing it for you."

"Don't!" said Liz and Toby in unison.

"All right, all right. The point is, I think Jesus was terrific but I don't buy the whole savior-redemption thing. You've got a sauce trail on your chin there, pal."

Rith grabbed the napkin off his lap and wiped all around his mouth. The spaghetti was good. The sauce had something extra in it.

"Dad, you always say I should have an open mind," said Toby. "So don't you think it's close-minded to say everyone at every church is trying to brainwash people?"

"Another point," said Liz, licking her finger and marking it in the air. "We always figured you'd want to explore at some point, Toby. Just not this soon."

"If I had my choice, you'd wait till you were in your twenties and had a few courses in critical thinking," said Eric.

"I'm advanced for my age," said Toby. "And look, I've got Rith to protect me from the brainwashing. If I start to believe too much, he'll notice."

"Rith, you're being used as a pawn in our family argument," said Liz. "Is that okay?"

"As long as I don't get in trouble for it," said Rith.

Eric laughed again, and Liz smiled and passed him the spaghetti. They called it an argument but it didn't feel that way. It was friendly and had extra flavor, just like the spaghetti sauce. The Corbetts all talked so fast Rith could hardly keep up. He'd had no idea that God was something you could argue about. You either did what they said and had faith or you were a heathen. Saved or not-saved, in or out.

"Rith, Toby says he's learning a thing or two in confirmation class," said Eric. "How about you? Do you learn anything there? Get any new ideas?"

"Not as much as here," said Rith, and Eric and Liz both laughed again.

"Hey, I've got a new idea," said Toby. "How about Rith and I have dessert upstairs? I think we've had enough of you guys for now."

"Go on, get out of here," said Eric. "We were tired of you anyway."

Toby grabbed a handful of cookies from the counter and Rith followed.

"Sorry about them," said Toby over his shoulder on the way up the stairs. "They're not normal, but we're free now. They both hate computer games, so they won't even come in the room, I promise."

Several hours later, Rith lay in the semi-dark on a cot next to Toby's bed. The house was quiet. Liz and Eric had said good night a while ago. Toby might even be asleep already. Probably he was.

"Toby," Rith whispered softly.

"Yeah?"

Not asleep. Now he had to say something.

"What?" asked Toby.

Rith's heart thumped and he swallowed hard.

"If I tell you something, promise you won't think I'm crazy?"

"How can I promise that when I don't know what you're going to say? I mean, if you say, Hey Tobe, let's dive out the window naked, I'm gonna think you're crazy."

Toby propped himself on his elbow, his shadow silhouetted by the glow from a dragon night light. "Come on, tell me," he said. "I won't think you're crazy."

"It's weird," warned Rith. "And you can't tell anybody."

"Cross my heart," said Toby. "No telling. We can spit and shake if you want."

The furnace hummed in the darkness and Toby waited.

Finally, Rith said, "What if I said that sometimes in the

middle of the night my house has a different set of stairs? They're wood instead of carpet, and they go around in a spiral."

Toby shifted to a sitting position, cross-legged on the edge of the bed.

"Ahhh, if you said that then I'd ask you if you ever went down them."

"What if I said yes? And at the bottom, the house isn't there. It's something different."

"I'd say it's a cool story. And I'd ask you if you were making it up on the spot or did you think of it earlier."

"What if I said I wasn't making it up?"

"Well, honestly, I wouldn't be sure. Because I don't know you that well yet. But I'd want you to keep telling me about it anyway."

Rith looked up at the biggest dragon, the one over the foot of Toby's bed. The shadow of its wings stretched on the ceiling, reaching out toward Rith. He could just keep telling it this way. A story. Maybe true, maybe not.

"There's an old guy down there sitting by the fire. And he's got a cat."

"What is he, like a wizard?"

"Mm, no. Not a wizard. He reads from the Bible."

Toby laughed. "Okay, come on. For real. You're totally making this up, aren't you?"

Rith swallowed hard. This was where he should say, *Yeah, great story, huh? And how about that Bible twist?* The silence stretched out.

"Maybe I am," he finally said. "But maybe not. I told

you it was weird."

"Well keep going. Either way, it's good. What's the guy read out of the Bible?"

"It's how he talks," said Rith. "He reads stuff. Like, he read me this thing, a good name is better than precious ointment. And speaking the truth is honest evidence. That's how I knew to say no to changing my name. And last time he read something about dog vomit."

"What? Dog vomit? There's no dog vomit in the Bible."

"I bet there is. I just can't remember where he said it was. I remembered the verse of the name thing and it was actually there. Right where he said."

"Wow. No wonder you thought I'd think you were crazy. This is wild. If you're making this up then you're a creative genius. Are you a genius?"

"No," said Rith. "I've never gotten better than a B in math. Besides, where would I get the Bible stuff? I never heard that verse about a good name before. Or the dog vomit one."

"Dog vomit." Toby reached over to turn on the lamp. "Let's Google it."

Rith watched over Toby's shoulder as he typed in "dog vomit Bible."

The first hit was "Proverbs 26:11. *As a dog that returns to his vomit, so is a fool that repeats his folly.*"

"That's it!" yelled Rith. "It is, I remember, that's what he said. Proverbs."

Toby spun around in his chair. "You know what that means, don't you? It means it's real! You couldn't make that up. You don't even believe in God."

"I know," said Rith. "If I was going to make something up, it wouldn't have anything to do with a Bible."

"Hey! Maybe the old guy *is* God."

"I thought about that," said Rith. "But why would God have to read the stuff? It's supposed to be his word so why wouldn't he just say it?"

"Good point. Hey, can I come over next weekend? I want to see this guy."

"We can try it," said Rith. "But he never comes when I want him to. I set my alarm a few times and he was never there. He only comes when I'm not expecting him."

"Boys!" called Liz. "Time to settle down in there. Lights off."

Toby turned off the computer and they both got back in bed.

"What else does he say?" asked Toby.

"Lots of stuff. Like when I told him I don't like Walt, he said, 'He who conceals hatred has lying lips.'"

"Huh," said Toby. "Lying lips. I like that one. But aren't you supposed to hide it if you hate someone? You know, if you can't say anything nice don't say anything at all?"

"That's what I thought," said Rith. "But the other day I thought about lying lips and the honest evidence thing, and that's when I told them I didn't want to change my name, and it totally worked."

"Hey, that's great! So this Bible guy told you how to keep the comet."

They both lay quietly for a moment, and then Toby said

in a perfect Yoda voice, "Lying lips have not. Vomit return to fool does do."

"Yeah," said Rith, laughing. "It's kinda like that."

"Dude, you are so lucky. The Force is with you."

Toby sat up and tapped the big dragon so it spun on its string. The shadow circled on the ceiling overhead, shrinking and stretching its wings as it went around.

Lucky. That was one way Rith had never thought about himself. Not once. Ever.

Since he'd been at Toby's the night before, Rith had completely forgotten that it was Super Bowl Sunday. That's all Walt could talk about when they sat down to dinner after church.

"My money's on the underdog," said Walt, rubbing his hands together over the pork chop on his plate. "How about you, Rith? You'll probably want to catch a nap before the game. I suppose you and your pal stayed up goofing off all night."

"Not really," said Rith, shrugging.

"Meow," said Emma. "Meow meow meow."

"That's right, girlie," said Walt. "And what does a doggie say?"

"Meow."

"She's on such a kitty kick lately," said Mom, shaking her head.

Rith looked hard at Emma, remembering the kitty fit she'd had in the grocery store. She stared at him, eyes blue and clear.

"Super Bowl starts at five-thirty," said Mom. "We'll order in pizza."

"Can I be excused?" said Rith.

"You are going to watch with us, aren't you?" asked Mom.

"Mm, maybe," he said, pushing his chair back and taking his plate to the sink.

Lying lips maybe, but too bad. The only thing worse than watching the Stupor Bowl with Walt was talking about why he wouldn't watch the Stupor Bowl with Walt. He headed up to the quiet safety of his room.

Two years earlier, Mom had been pregnant with Emma and sick and she made Rith go along with Walt to Uncle Don's to watch. He might have watched if he'd been home just to see the good commercials, but he didn't care one thing about the game. Don and Walt and Ty jumped up and down and yelled at the screen, and everyone chowed on Aunt Janeen's nachos and cheese and crackers and dips. Walt and Don shared a six-pack of beer and Ty downed sodas. Rith sat in the corner on a beanbag chair with his arms crossed, mad that he had to be there and bored with football. Then it came time to get in the car and go home.

"My dad got killed by someone like you," Rith had said to Walt as they stood in the entry way. "You shouldn't drink and drive."

Walt's already red face got darker. He plucked Rith's jacket off the hook and tossed it to him, saying, "Put it on."

Rith let the jacket drop to the floor. He was making a

stand for his dad. He crossed his arms and planted his feet.

"No," he said. "I'm not going anywhere with a drunk driver."

Walt stood and looked at him, slowly shaking his head.

"Buddy boy, for a nickel I'd tell you a thing or two," Walt said.

Rith didn't budge and he didn't look away. His heart thumped so hard he could barely breathe. Would Walt hit him? Walt turned away, cracked his knuckles, took a deep breath and turned back.

"Here's the deal, Rith," he said. "I've had a few but I'm not drunk. If I were drunk, you'd know it. Put your jacket on and let's go."

Rith held his ground, staring at Walt.

"Pick it up," repeated Walt. "Right now."

Make me, Rith thought, slitting his eyes.

Walt stepped closer, bent over and picked the jacket up. He leaned out and yanked Rith's legs from under him, sweeping him up and cradling him like a baby. Rith struggled silently but Walt had him clamped tight, arms pinned to his sides.

"Someone come and open the door," Walt yelled.

Ty appeared, and Rith had a glimpse of his wide-eyed face as Walt swept out the door with Rith.

"Bye, Ty," said Walt, his beery breath over Rith's face.

"Bye, Uncle Walt."

The door closed behind them. Walt carried Rith over to the car and set him down, holding him by the back of the collar as he unlocked the door.

"Now get in there," he said, letting go of him with a shove. "And don't ever make me humiliate you like that again." He threw Rith's jacket on the floor of the car. Rith got in and sat tight against the door, as far away from Walt as he could get. Tears spilled out and burned down his cheeks. He refused to move to brush them away or wipe his nose. Walt didn't say one word to him and when they got home, Rith left the jacket in the car and went directly to his room. He didn't come out until morning and when he did, he knew. Walt hated him and he hated Walt. And that was that.

Rith stretched out on his bed, staring at the ceiling. Why couldn't Mom have met someone fun like Toby's dad? Or better yet, why couldn't his dad come back? He'd come to the door and Rith wouldn't know him but he'd know Rith and he'd grin and Mom would run screaming over and they'd hug and spin around in a circle and pull Rith in, and the three of them would go off and leave Walt standing there with his big stupid mouth hanging open and . . .

Mom knocked on his door.

"Rith, are you awake? The pizza's here."

He wrenched his eyes open. The bedroom was dark.

"Not hungry," he said.

"Are you sure? Come on down, Rith. Watch with us for a little while."

"Too tired," he said.

He felt her outside his door, waiting. Hoping. He held

his breath, not quite knowing if he wanted her to come in or not.

"Okay," she finally said. "But don't stay up all night reading."

Her footsteps went off down the hall and Rith let his breath out. She didn't really want him to come downstairs. The happy Kurth family was much better off without him there.

Whatever Mom and Walt had been arguing about the week before, it wasn't over. As Rith came down the stairs early Monday morning, he heard the voices and stopped on the landing.

"Don't pressure me, Walt. This is my decision."

"Not if you really want me to be his father. Starting off with a lie doesn't set right. A boy should know where he comes from."

Rith's breath caught on its way in, almost choking him. Walt definitely knew something.

"Walt, stop." Mom had tears on her voice now. "I need more time. It's only been a couple of weeks."

"Okay." A chair scraped on the tiles. "Fine, more time. But the longer you wait, the worse it's going to be. It's not fair to anybody. You just let me know when you're done taking all that time."

Walt's footsteps moved across the tile. Rith edged around the corner to the stair above the landing so he wouldn't be seen as Walt crossed the living room. Footsteps sounded on the entryway tile. Coat on, front door open, close, lock.

Rith went back up to his room for about ten minutes. He thudded his feet on the way downstairs and coughed loudly at the landing. When he stepped into the kitchen, Mom had her back to him, looking for something in the refrigerator.

"Hi honey. You must be caught up on your sleep, you're down here early."

"I guess. Everything okay?"

She turned and looked him over. Trying to see if he'd heard anything. He kept his face blank, just like hers.

"Everything's fine," she said. "What do you want for breakfast?"

"Just some cereal."

She set the bowl in front of him and crossed over to the sink, not meeting his eye.

"Anything you want to tell me, Mom?"

She opened the dishwasher and started unloading it, clinking plates into the cupboard.

"Make sure you dress warm today, it's cold outside."

Lying lips.

Toby popped up at Rith's locker before the first bell on Monday.

"Did he come?"

"No," said Rith.

"Well, be sure and tell me next time he does. Hey, my Mom and Dad liked you a lot.

"Really? Why?"

"My dad likes you because you're a heathen, of course. And my mom said," Toby fake-smiled, batting his eyes, "'that Rith is very sweet.'"

"Shut up," said Rith, turning away. But warmth spread around him like the heat from Bible Man's fire, and the feeling stayed with him all day as he moved from one class to the next. Maybe he should tell Mom he knew she was hiding something and ask her what it was. So far he was two for two on speaking truth.

The principal made an announcement last period over the intercom about the wind-chill warnings. Fifteen minutes to frostbite on exposed skin. Rith ran from the school building to the bus and sat as close to the heater as he could get. The cold pushed against the bus windows and wiggled up through the floor, chilling his feet. A few light flakes blew on the gray breeze.

Rith studied Mom and Walt through dinner. They didn't say much, just "Pass the butter" and "Is there more meat?" He helped clear the table, hoping to get Mom alone and ask her. But between the dark circles under her eyes and the way she thanked him for helping clean up, he couldn't do it. She took the kids to get their baths, and he went upstairs and called Toby.

"So do you still think I'm not crazy?" he asked.

"Still not sure," said Toby. "But you know what, I thought of something. Eragon, Harry Potter, Luke Skywalker, none of them had dads. And then weird stuff happens and they find out about their dad. Could this Bible guy be your dad?"

"No, too old. My dad would be my mom's age. This guy is really, really old."

"Oh. Hey, are you sure he's not God?"

"Do you really believe in God? All the way?"

"Sure I do." Toby's answer was that quick. "I never really thought of him as an old guy in your basement—"

"Not the basement. He's where the living room oughta be."

"Okay, living room. I'm not so sure about the whole Jesus part yet but I definitely believe in God. My dad says God is a feeling. My mom says God is love and you can put that in any shape you want."

"For not being religious people, your parents sure talk about God a lot."

"Yeah, I guess they do. I pray to get what I want even though my dad says that's insulting to God, to pray for a snowboard. I don't see why. God can just not pick up, you know? So I leave him a voice mail for when he has time to get around to it."

"How can you be insulting to a feeling, if God's just a feeling?"

"See," said Toby. "My dad doesn't make any more sense than anyone else does. Do you really not believe in God? At all?"

Rith let the phone line hum in silence. Sometimes, just a little, he did. "Mostly not," he finally said.

"Your Bible Man sounds like who I'd want God to be if he came down here and hung around with us. Have you ever heard that song about what if God was a stranger on the bus? It's a great song. Hey, can I come over this weekend? I really want to see this guy. Maybe he'll give me a snowboard."

Bible Man was Rith's. Toby had a dad. Rith had Bible Man.

"Unless you think it'd mess things up," said Toby. "Break the spell or whatever."

"I'll think about it. Anyway, I gotta check with my mom. Something's up between her and Walt. He wants her to tell me something and she doesn't want to. I think it's something about my dad."

"I thought Walt wanted to erase him off the face of the earth."

"He does. That's why I don't get it. I'm going to try and trap my mom tomorrow before school and make her tell me."

"Well, good luck. Let me know what happens. Hey, can you hear that wind outside? It sounds like a hurricane."

Rith got up and pushed the curtain aside. The naked branches outside his window moved stiffly, silhouetted against the streetlight. The wind whistled and slithered around the house, skritching claws creeping across the glass, looking for a way in. He let the curtain drop.

"Looks cold out there," he said.

"Let me know about this weekend, okay? Talk to you later."

Rith set the phone down and his door banged open. It was Emma in her one-piece pink fuzzy sleeper, running in like she owned the place.

"Elmo love you," she yelled.

"Emma, get out of here," said Rith, reaching down to grab her.

She squirmed away from him and wiggle-crawled under his bed before he could get a hand on so much as a plastic-bottomed foot.

"Kitty," she called.

Rith sank to the floor, lying down and looking into the darkness beneath the bed.

"Hey Emma, do you know a kitty?" asked Rith. "A gray kitty?"

"Elmo love you."

Rith rolled his eyes. Kitty, Elmo, she just said whatever she heard.

"Come on, Emma, get out of there."

He grabbed for her and she moved out of reach. He slammed his fist on the floor and Emma burbled out a laugh. Rith reached again for her foot and got air. He stood up and paced, and then, struck by inspiration, stuck a CD in and turned up the volume.

Sure enough, Emma's head popped out from under the bed. Rith looked away and shuffled his feet back and forth, pretending he had forgotten about her. Emma ran over and started her giant-step dance, grinning up at him.

Rith leaned down and scooped her up, holding her in a tight cradle so she couldn't wiggle out. He took her out into the hall, set her down, and then ran back in his room and locked the door behind him. She pounded on the door and screamed. Rith turned up the music.

Rith counted over a thousand sheep try-ing to get to sleep that night. He lay with-out moving, not even to scratch an itchy toe, for what seemed like four hours but turned out to be sev-enteen minutes. Sleep had left his life forever and taken Bible Man with it; he was doomed to lie there until morn-ing and again the next night until morning and again and again. And just as he was explaining to Mom why he kept falling asleep in school, he woke up. Wide awake. 2:47.

The cat met Rith at the bottom of the stairs. Flames licked over the logs, pulling him toward the fireplace. Bible Man looked up as Rith came around in front of the chair, and a slight change in expression passed over his worn face. A shadow of a smile.

"You came back!" said Rith. "It's been a whole week. I thought maybe you wouldn't come back. Anyway, I did it. I spoke truth to Walt. What do you think of that?"

"Light is sweet," nodded Bible Man, "and it is pleasant for the eyes to behold the sun. Ecclesiastes eleven seven."

"Yeah, I couldn't believe it. I thought my mom was going to be mad but she wasn't at all. And Walt, when he looked at me and said 'fair enough,' it was, I don't know, almost like he respected me."

"A wise son makes a glad father, but a foolish son is a sorrow to his mother. Proverbs ten one."

"Yeah, but Walt's not my father. Hey, do you know my dad?"

Rith waited for an answer, hoping, not really believing. But still hoping. Bible Man didn't make a move to flip any pages.

"My mom and Walt are fighting about something," said Rith, trying a different direction. "I think it's got something to do with me. Do you know what it is?"

Bible Man sat perfectly still like he was in a trance.

"How about the adoption thing? They aren't going to make me change my name, but I still want to ditch the whole deal. You got any ideas about that?"

"Even a child makes himself known by his acts, whether what he does is pure and right," Bible Man said immediately. He didn't even look down at the Bible. "Proverbs twenty eleven."

Rith drummed his fingers on the hearth.

"Yeah, sure, so I want to do it pure and right. But how?"

Bible Man stared into the flames. Rith waited. The cat sat upright like an Egyptian statue, watching Rith's every move.

"Hey," said Rith, flapping his hand. "Did you hear me?

About ditching adoption?"

Nothing. The old guy didn't even blink. He just sat there.

"Can't you just talk sometimes? Do you have to take everything out of the Bible? I mean, what if you want to say something that isn't in there?"

"A wise son hears his father's instruction," Bible Man said, still not blinking or moving. "Proverbs thirteen one."

"Yeah, that's real easy if you have a father to give you instruction," Rith said. "Which I don't happen to have, remember?"

Bible Man closed the Bible. He looked hard at Rith, his eyes narrowed behind the thick glass. He spoke very softly.

"Be angry but sin not. Psalms four four."

Rith felt suddenly cold and wrapped his arms around himself.

"Hey look, I'm sorry," he said. "Don't get mad at me, okay? The father thing just gets to me sometimes."

Bible Man nodded slowly and took off his glasses. He set them on the closed Bible on his lap and, holding Rith's eyes with his, he spoke very slowly.

"I have called you by name, you are mine. When you pass through the waters I will be with you; and through the rivers, they shall not overwhelm you; when you walk through fire you shall not be burned and the flame shall not consume you. Isaiah forty-three, one and two."

He nodded once more, then closed his eyes, settling back into the chair. He seemed to be instantly asleep, breathing deeply. Rith turned to the cat, who was sitting at his feet.

"Is he . . . is Bible Man God?"

The cat made a long and drawn-out growling noise, and looked pointedly at the stairs. Bible Man continued to breathe deeply.

"Do you think I could just stay for a while?" Rith whispered. "I won't mess with anything, I just want to sit here by the fire."

The cat glared at Rith, then looked at the stairs. Rith, stairs. Rith scooted closer to the fire. Those words. *I have called you by name, you are mine.* He wanted to hear them again, wanted to stay in the place where they'd been spoken. The flames were gone and the coals pulsed orange, breathing color in and out without much heat. He looked around for some wood to put on and warm things up. The cat growled again.

"Please, can't I stay?" asked Rith.

The cat stalked to Rith's side, its yellow eyes boring into his face and the end of its tail twitching.

"Okay, okay, don't get mad. I'm going," said Rith.

The cat followed him all the way to the foot of the spiral and sat, tail continuing to twitch as Rith backed up the stairs. When he got to his room, Rith switched the light on over his desk and pulled his notebook and Bible out. He found Isaiah 43 and carefully copied Bible Man's words. *I have called you by name, you are mine.*

Even when Bible Man looked mad or told him to sin not, he did it with that soft voice and those eyes that Rith could feel looking right into his heart. The words felt like Mom's B.W. hand on his face, telling him it was okay if he didn't understand the math. God or not, it was the best thing he'd found in a long time.

Rith read the quote again. What waters? What fire? Bible Man had looked so seriously at him, so directly, when he said that. Like he wanted to engrave it on Rith's brain. Rith chewed on his thumbnail and looked out at the moon on the snow. Maybe Bible Man was trying to warn him about something.

Rith woke up thinking about Bible Man. *Be angry but sin not.* What was the sin? Complaining about not having a father? That made about as much sense as the dog vomit thing.

At breakfast, Mom and Walt barely spoke. Mom's eye circles were even darker. She was about to crack. She couldn't hold up under the Walt pressure. Nobody could.

The TV on the counter was full of warnings about a snowstorm blowing in across the plains. A real old-fashioned blizzard, they said. Up to a foot of snow, maybe more. Rith hoped they wouldn't cancel school. Nothing worse than being stuck in the house all day. Unless maybe Walt tried to make him go snowmobiling, that would be worse.

Rith's bus got to school late, so he didn't have time to find Toby before homeroom. He ran up to the third floor after the last bell, looking up and down the crowded hallway for a spot of red hair. Just as he was about to give up, Rith spotted Toby coming out of the boys' bathroom.

"He came last night!" he said, skidding up behind Toby.

"So what'd he say? Anything more about dog vomit? Oh hey, did you ask him about getting me a snowboard?"

"He thought it was good that I ditched the curse of Kurth," said Rith. "And he said some other stuff, too. But I gotta run. I'll miss the bus."

"Call me tonight and tell me," said Toby. "No wait, we have to go to my grandma's tonight, it's her birthday. Catch me tomorrow at school, okay?"

Rith nodded and bumped Toby's fist, running for the stairs. On the bus on the way home, he pulled out the scrap of paper that he'd written Bible Man's last words on and read them to himself over and over again, memorizing them.

Rith couldn't get warm. He huddled farther under the covers, shivering. An eerie, frantic noise drilled into his brain, making him shiver harder. He put his hands over his ears, trying to make the cold and the sound go away, and his own movement woke him up. The cat yowled again.

Rith turned on his bedside light and sat up. His feet felt like ice cubes. Why was it so cold? He hurriedly put on the clothes from the floor beside his bed and grabbed another sweatshirt besides.

He opened his bedroom door, and the hall was colder still. The furnace must be broken. Walt never let the house get this cold. Rith didn't even think about the spiral staircase but when he found it, his heart thumped in his chest. Bible Man would know what was going on.

As Rith came down the stairs, the temperature dropped even further. The rough wooden door stood open and a cold wind swept into the dark room. He ran around in front of the armchair. It was empty. He reached into the fireplace and held his hand over the ashes. The fire was completely out, the fireplace cold. The only light came from the window and the doorway, and that wasn't even light. Just less darkness.

Rith ran over to shut the door. The snow that was drifting in stuck to his socks. He spotted a pair of big boots and slid into them, then kicked at the snow so he could close the door. He kicked something that wasn't snow, something that moved in a different way. He leaned over, brought a hand out from his armpit, and picked it up. A little rubber boot. He squinted, bringing it close to his face to see it better. Elmo looked back at him.

Rith looked out across the snow. A trail of dark dents led into the storm. Footprints. Clouds covered the moon and stars but the night glowed with light from the snow.

"Emma!" he yelled. "Emma, are you out there?"

The only response was the howl of the wind, throwing stinging snow against his cheeks and filling in the wavering line of tracks. Rith stepped back inside and shoved the door closed, looking around frantically. Where was Bible Man? What should he do? What world was outside the wooden door? If Bible Man was a dream, the dream was getting way out of hand.

A thick coat hung from a wooden peg next to the door. Rith put it on over his sweatshirt, and put on the cap with ear flaps that hung next to it. He opened the door again and stepped outside. Standing next to the small unlit cabin with his hands in his armpits, he squinted into the vast spread of snow-blowing darkness.

"Emma!" he called. The wind sucked the words out of his mouth and carried them away. Rith gasped. The cold pinched his nostrils coming in and hurt on its way to his lungs. His thighs were already numb as the wind whipped through his thin sweatpants. He stumbled as he stepped forward in the big boots, following Emma's tracks. The snow blew sideways. A few yards ahead of him, the faint indentations disappeared completely. He turned around and looked back. His own tracks were already drifting in behind him. Bible Man's cabin was a dark shadow huddled in the middle of gray and white. If he lost sight of it, he was in trouble.

"Emma!" he called again. "Emma, Emma!"

He shuffled through the snow, shivering and peering ahead. How could he find a baby in a snowstorm? He would get lost himself and then someone would have to save him. For the first time, Rith hoped with all his heart and all his strength that Bible Man was a dream.

He stopped and looked back at the cabin again. It was smaller now, farther away. Just a dark shape in the distance. Rith turned out toward the open field, trying to figure out which way Emma would go. The whole thing was crazy. It was his dream, so he just needed to go back to bed and it would be over. He started back toward the cabin, bringing his cold hands up to his mouth one at a time and blowing warm breath across his knuckles and down into the sleeve.

A high-pitched yowl stopped him in his tracks. It pierced through the howl of the wind and went directly to Rith's gut. He pulled the earflap up on one ear and turned slowly in place, trying to figure out where it came from.

Again it sounded. The cat. The cat was yowling. Rith dropped the earflap and walked toward the sound, searching the night for a glimpse of gray against the white. He fixed on a little rise in the snow and plodded toward it. The yowling continued like a beacon, pulling him on through the cold.

When Rith reached the rise, it turned out to be a lump in the snow. He nudged it with his foot. The yowling stopped. Rith looked down, and nudged again. He bent over and used the sleeve of the jacket to brush a layer of snow away. His breath caught in his chest. Forgetting about his cold hands, he dug and scraped at the snow.

Rith turned Emma over and gently brushed the snow off her face. His own hands were stiff, no feeling in his fingers. He called her name, tapped her on the cheek, and then plunged his frozen hands into the snow beneath her, gathering her to his chest. He struggled to his feet with Emma in his arms. The boots seemed to fit better, less clumsy as he ran through the knee-deep snow. Emma was dead weight and he struggled, ten more steps and then ten more steps. As he approached the dark distant shape of the cabin, it grew to a two-story house.

He stumbled onto the patio and found the sliding glass door open a crack. He wedged his boot in and shoved, then turned sideways to squeeze through with Emma. The kitchen was dark.

"Mom!" he yelled. "Mom, Walt, Mom, wake up!"

He ran clomping in his boots, around the table, into the living room, down the hallway, knocking the doorknob with his elbow and shoving into the master bedroom. He set Emma on the end of the king-size bed, still yelling, and the lights came on.

"Rith, what's wrong?"

Mom was already sitting up. Walt emerged sleepily from under the covers.

"It's Emma, she was outside, I found her in the snow."

"Oh my God."

Rith took a step back as Mom scrambled to lean over Emma. His knees trembled from exhaustion and fear and his skin burned from the cold. Mom put her cheek up close to Emma, her face turned toward Rith, her eyes wide and scared. She turned to Walt, who was already punching numbers on the phone.

"Walt, she's not breathing. And she's so cold . . ."

"Yes, it's an emergency!" Walt barked into the phone. "My daughter, she's frozen, she was out in the snow. She'll be two in March. Walter Kurth, 64 Spring Lake Road . . . Don't know, my son just brought her in, no, not breathing. Wait, let me check."

Walt put his big, thick finger on the side of Emma's neck. He moved his finger around, searching.

"Come on, baby," he said. "God, come on, you have to . . . Can't find any," he said into the phone. "Nope, can't feel anything. A sleeper, a sleeper with feet. Nope, nothing else."

Mom held Emma close, pulling the white chenille bedspread around her little body. Rith's hands hurt. He rubbed his fingers together and couldn't feel the skin, just a deep aching around the bones. He put both hands up to his mouth, breathing warm air on them. The skin on the front of his thighs tingled, thawing back to life.

"Put her on the floor," Walt said. "Hard surface, we gotta do CPR, come on now. Open her sleeper so you can get at her chest, hurry up."

Walt relayed instructions from the phone and Mom followed them. Rith took another step back. Emma was so white. Glassy white. Plastic white. No pulse, she was dead. He was too late, too slow.

"Rith, go get the front door open," said Walt. "They'll be here any minute."

Rith ran across the carpeting in the living room, same no-color as the stairs. Across the big squares of ceramic tile in the wide entryway. He threw the front door open and wind and snow swirled in, whipping around his face. A fire truck and two police cars came wailing into the driveway.

"In here, in here, in here!" Rith screamed, his voice cracking. Red lights flashed around and around through the snow, and dark shapes hustled up the driveway.

"Where's the baby?"

"This way." Rith ran back to the bedroom. The firefighters moved in, a woman gently guiding Mom back and kneeling over Emma, a man introducing himself to Walt.

Uniforms and radios and a big equipment bag immediately surrounded Emma. Rith backed up until he bumped into the rocking chair and sank into it. A shiver ran through him, and then another. Not cold shivers—the room was hot and he still a coat on. Ben hollered from the nursery.

"Excuse me, son."

Rith jumped out of the chair. A very tall policeman loomed over him.

"No, relax. Sit back down there." The cop put a hand on Rith's shoulder and pressed him back into the chair. He pulled a footstool over from the corner of the room and sat on it, his long legs folded in front of him, a notebook resting on his knee.

"My name's Tim. I'm a police officer. And your name is . . . ?"

"Rith. Rith Haley."

"Right, Rith. Your dad says you're the—"

"Stepfather," corrected Rith.

The cop glanced over at Walt, who stood watching the firefighters work on Emma.

"Okay, stepfather," said Tim. "Now he says . . ."

The paramedics burst into the room, carrying more gear.

"Come on, let's go," called the first one. He moved in, picked Emma up off the floor, and ran out the door with her. Rith stood, thinking to follow. The police officer reached up and put a heavy hand on his shoulder.

"Hang on there, fella," he said. "You can't go in the ambulance."

"But what about . . ."

"Hang on. We'll all follow along in a minute."

Mom pulled on a sweater and told Walt to get Ben. Walt rushed into the nursery, followed by another officer. Ben stopped screaming. The radios squawked and the firefighters packed up the equipment bag. Walt reappeared in the doorway with Ben wrapped in a blanket.

"Let's go," he said.

Tim stepped over and talked with another officer, then turned to Mom.

"Do you mind if Rith rides with me?" he asked. "If I can get his statement on the way to the hospital, it'll save us all some time."

"That's fine," said Mom, without even looking at Rith. He opened his mouth to say something, but she followed Walt and two of the officers out the door, and suddenly only Rith and Tim were left in the room.

Rith's hands still burned with the heat of thawing. He opened and closed them, feeling warmth move through the joints. He looked at the sleeve of his jacket. His blue down jacket. Where was Bible Man's old brown coat? He looked down at his feet. He was wearing his own boots, not the big ones at Bible Man's door.

"You okay?" asked Tim. "Must've been pretty cold out there."

"What do you mean, my statement?" asked Rith.

"You just need to tell me what happened," said Tim, "since you found her. It's no big thing, really. You tell me everything, I write it down, and then you sign it."

Rith suddenly felt dizzy. Which everything? Which everything was he supposed to tell?

"Hey there, fella," said Tim. "You probably need to catch your breath, huh? Why don't you take off that coat a minute, have a drink of water or something? We'll get to the hospital soon enough. I'll use the siren."

Rith wanted to leave right away but his legs were still shaking so badly that he had to sit down. He perched on the edge of the bed.

"Is Emma dead?" he asked.

"I don't know. Depends on lots of things. She's getting the best care around, you know. Medics got here in a hurry, we got CPR up and going, and little kids have a lot of bounce back."

"Can we just go?" Rith asked.

"Not until I'm sure you're not going to pass out on me," said Tim. "You're looking a little peaked. Why don't you lie down, or at least lean over and put your head between your knees. Once I see some blood in your face, we can go."

Rith didn't want to lie down. He slid to the floor, drew his knees up in front of him, and put his face down on them. He felt Tim looking at him. What would he say? That he had a bad dream and then it turned into real life? That his sister followed an imaginary cat that he just happened to imagine, too?

"Rith?" Tim dropped a hand on his shoulder, shaking it a little. "How you doing?"

Rith stayed in the darkness behind his eyelids for a moment more, looking there for some kind of answer. Some instruction. He got nothing. Tim shook his shoulder again, and he opened his eyes and looked up.

"Okay, that's better," said Tim. "You got a little color in your cheeks now. Do you think you're okay to go?"

Rith nodded and Tim gave him a warm hand, pulling him to his feet. Rith glanced around as they passed through the living room. Leather furniture, coffee table, TV. No stone hearth, no wooden mantel, no old man. Just the no-color carpet stretching everywhere, across the living room and up the stairs, all the way to his room. No wooden spiral. No Bible. Maybe Walt was right. Maybe he didn't know what reality was.

Tim's radio squawked behind him.

"Yeah?" Tim said into it, pausing.

Rith opened the front door and stepped out into the cold. He felt the wind's bite again, but its teeth weren't so sharp with the lights of the house all around. He listened for a yowl from the cat but heard only the lonely whine of the wind. Tim stepped up next to him, pulling the door closed.

"Rith, did you hear?" he said, putting an arm around Rith's shoulders and guiding him to the police car. "They found a pulse on the way to the hospital."

Rith looked up at him sharply, not daring to believe it. Tim nodded.

"When someone gets real cold it seems like they shut down all the way but they don't. The core stays warm. You got her inside fast enough, it looks like she's going to be okay."

Tim opened the door of the police car, and Rith slid into the passenger seat. He leaned his head back, letting his breath all the way out for the first time. She wasn't dead.

Rith came around the corner to the hospital waiting room and stopped short, Tim running into him from behind. Mom held Ben in her arms and Walt sat close, his arm around her shoulders. Mom looked up and saw Rith frozen in the doorway. She handed Ben to Walt and came over, putting her arms around Rith and pulling him into the room.

"Rith, are you all right? I'm sorry, I didn't know we would be so far ahead of you. What happened? Are you okay?"

"How's Emma?"

"We think she's going to be all right. They have this machine called a Thermal Angel, it warms the fluid going into her body and warms her up.

"They're not dead until they're warm and dead," said Rith.

"What?" said Mom, pulling back.

Tim stepped forward. "That's what I told him on the way here. I explained how cold and not breathing doesn't necessarily mean dead."

"He's right. they found a pulse on the way here, Rith. They don't think her heart ever really stopped, it was just so faint we couldn't feel it. We can go in and see her again in a few minutes."

Tim put his big hand on Rith's shoulder again.

"All right, fella," he said. "Thanks for all your help. You're the hero of the day, you know."

Tim gave Rith's shoulder a squeeze and moved over to Walt.

"Sorry to bother you, Mr. and Mrs. Haley, but I need to get your statements too."

Walt's eyes flicked to Rith, then back to Tim. He passed Ben to Mom, and stood.

"Kurth," he said, putting out his hand. "Walter Kurth. Let's get this over with, can we?"

As the sun came up and the day went on, Rith told his story to Mom and Walt, and he told it to the doctor. Then he had to tell it again to several of the nurses, and to some other people in the waiting room. He told about finding the door open, seeing Emma's Elmo boot, and going outside to look for her. He told about finding her and thinking she was dead, struggling to pick her up and run through the snow with her. He told about the foot-prints that led him out the door. He didn't mention any-thing about the yowling cat that led him to the rise in the snow. He didn't bring up the fact that he had gone out the door in one set of jacket, boots, and hat, and come in with a different set.

The waiting room emptied around noon and Rith stretched out on the couch, closing his eyes. The next thing he knew, Mom was shaking his shoulder.

"Rith. Rith honey, wake up."

He jerked out of a dark dream of swirling snow.

"Is Emma—?"

"No, she's fine. They're going to keep her overnight and I'm staying with her. Do you want to stay with Toby tonight? Walt has to go in to work for a while. He's taking Ben over to Uncle Don's."

"Yeah, Toby's," he said, blinking himself awake.

"I called and talked to his mom while you were asleep," said Mom. "She said it was fine, she's off work today and can come and pick you up here."

While Mom called back to make arrangements, Rith went in to see Emma.

"Rit," she said, her eyes bright blue in the midst of all the white.

Something curious twisted in Rith's chest, like a live thing gripping and squeezing. He took a shaky breath and swallowed. He reached out to touch a yellow curl.

"Hey Emma, you just rest up and get better, okay?"

He turned to see Mom smiling at him in the doorway. She grabbed him as he went by, holding his face between her hands.

"I love you, Rith," she said. "I'm so proud of you."

She pulled him in tight for a hug and the thing in his chest twisted sideways. What was she hiding from him?

Liz picked him up at the front entrance to the hospital. Piles of freshly plowed snow lined the streets, making huge white banks. The sun shone brightly but it was a brittle light, making icy blue shadows everywhere. Rith strapped himself into the front seat with the heater blowing on his feet and face. He was so tired he could barely keep his eyes open. Liz didn't ask questions; she put on some soft music and drove to his house so he could pick up things for school the next day.

"Do you want me to come in with you?" she asked as they pulled into the driveway.

"No, it's okay."

Rith ran up to the door, pulling the warm key out of his pocket. He let himself in, closing the cold off behind him. The living room stretched out before him, smooth and quiet, no-color. The house was completely quiet, waiting. He kicked off his boots and padded sock-footed across the tiled entryway.

Everything was clean and still. Rith checked the kitchen. The glass door was closed and locked. Emma's Elmo boot lay on the tile floor in a puddle. Hands in his pockets, Rith leaned into the door, resting his forehead on the cold glass. A smooth white drift fingered across the patio. Somewhere out there under the snow was Emma's other boot. But where was the cat? Did Emma go into Bible Man's world, or did the cat come into hers?

When he closed his eyes, Rith could still hear the cat yowls over the howl of the wind. Behind his eyelids he saw Emma's cold white face, felt the fear that was still in his stomach, the awful silence of Emma who never shut up for ten seconds.

He yanked himself away from the glass, shivering. Liz was waiting. He hurried upstairs and shoved his books into a backpack, threw clothes in his gym bag, and ran back downstairs. He looked back at the living room. Where was Bible Man? The door had been open. Had he gone out in the storm too?

When Rith came out of the steamy bathroom after a long hot shower, Toby was waiting on the other side of the door.

"So you're kinda like a hero now," he said. "Are you okay? What happened?"

Rith glanced at the stairs to see if Toby's parents were around.

"It was the cat," he whispered.

Toby grabbed him by the elbow and pulled him into the dragon room, shutting the door behind them.

"What was?"

"Tobe, I woke up and it was Bible Man's place but the door was open. And I found Emma's boot and I followed but I never would've found her if the cat hadn't kept yowling. It led me to her. But listen, I went outside in Bible Man's coat and boots, and then they turned into my own."

"Rith, how can that be? I mean, how can that be?"

"I don't know, Toby. I thought Bible Man was just my thing. Not made up exactly but not real. Like, not *real*

real. Now I don't know what to think."

"Why didn't Bible Man stop her?"

"He wasn't there. I think she was trying to follow the cat. She's been all on a kitty kick ever since this started, and I kept thinking it was a coincidence."

Rith stopped, staring out Toby's bedroom window at the brittle cold. The sun was starting to go down, a fade of yellow in the western sky. The trees shivered in the wind, dropping little poofs of snow.

"I'm kinda scared, Toby. Maybe I really am crazy."

"Your sister following the cat out in a blizzard, that's scary," said Toby. "We should tell my dad."

"No," Rith turned to Toby and shook his head hard. "He'd tell my mom and she'll freak out completely. Or Walt. He already thinks there's something wrong with me."

"Hey, this is my dad, he's half crazy himself. And really Rith, I'm kinda scared too. I think we should tell him. He won't tell anyone."

"What if he does?"

"I'm telling you, he won't. He knows how to keep his mouth shut. He doesn't even tell my mom stuff if I tell him not to."

"How do you know?"

"I've tested."

Rith looked out the window again. He wasn't going to cry but he didn't want Toby to see him trying not to. Everything was too much. Bible Man, Mom's secret, the blizzard and Emma and the cat and not knowing which parts belonged where. He was beyond tired.

"Okay," he said once he trusted his voice. "Okay, let's tell him. Not your mom though. Just him."

Eric sat in the rocking chair in the corner of Toby's bedroom and listened without interrupting. He nodded, his eyes fixed on Rith's face. Rith started with the first time he saw the wooden stairs and ended with the realization that he had his own jacket on.

"So?" asked Toby, who'd been bouncing a knee up and down the whole time Rith talked. "What is it? What's this Bible guy?"

Eric got up and walked over to the window, pulling the blinds closed against the darkness. Rith gave Toby a questioning look, turning his palms up. Toby shrugged. Finally Eric turned around and looked at Rith.

"The universe is full of strange things," he said. "Sounds like you bumped into one."

"But what is it?" asked Toby.

"I don't know," said Eric.

"Dad!" said Toby, his voice jumping an octave. "Come on, we need more than that. I mean, if it's leading a baby out in the snow, maybe it's ... I don't know ... evil. What if he's evil?"

"Is he evil, Rith?" asked Eric.

Rith thought of the old man's pale blue gaze, the warmth of the fire. The cat's fur. He shook his head.

"Well," said Eric. "There you go."

"But what if I'm wrong?" asked Rith.

"Are you?" asked Eric.

"I don't know. What if I'm crazy?"

The questions skip-hopped between the two of them and Toby's eyes followed, one side to the other.

"You seem like you've got a pretty good grip on reality. But it's good you're talking about it, checking it out. What about telling your parents?"

"No," Rith shook his head hard. "Please don't tell them, okay? They'd never get it. They'd want to lock me up. Or I don't know, maybe make me tell Pastor Paul about it. And Bible Man, he's mine. Private. Besides, Toby said you wouldn't tell. He promised."

Eric glanced sideways at Toby.

"Toby shouldn't promise things for me. But I won't tell anyone, not unless things start to seem dangerous or like you might get hurt."

"But wasn't this dangerous?" asked Toby.

"The blizzard was dangerous. All we know for sure is Emma went outside. It happens. I read something about a two-year-old in Canada last winter, he died because nobody found him in time. Emma didn't die because Rith got there. That's a good thing. Not evil."

Rith felt the rightness of that all the way from the inside out. "So could Bible Man be God?" he asked.

"Who knows?" said Eric. "I like to say that God's not an old white man but what do I know? No more than you do."

Rith looked down at his hands knitted together between his knees.

"Rith, is there something you want me to do?" asked Eric. "I'll try to help you work things through the best I can. If we decide together that you need to tell your folks or someone else, I'd back you on that too."

"No." Rith shook his head hard again. "No, I guess I'll . . . I don't know. I still can't figure out how Emma got into it. I don't see how that could happen."

"We don't know if Emma really was in it, or if she went outside for some other reason. Maybe she saw the same things you did, maybe not. Maybe you've got a powerful creative mind—and I do *not* mean," he said, holding up his finger to stop Toby's opening mouth, "that you're making this up. At least, not in the way people usually mean that. I mean the human mind and spirit are amazingly complex, beyond anything I understand. And you, Orithian Haley, maybe have an extra dollop of complexity."

"So you don't think I'm crazy?"

"Nope, I don't think so. Keep talking about it to Toby here, or to me. If you start sounding crazy, we'll tell you. Okay?"

"Okay." Rith nodded.

"You look like you've been run over by a truck," said Eric. "Come on down and have some dinner. Then you're going to bed, forget about that confirmation class. Toby's going to come down and watch TV with us and let you sleep."

Toby opened his mouth again, and Eric stopped it with another upraised finger.

"No negotiating," he said.

Rith did go to sleep right after dinner and slept solidly and dreamlessly. He woke to Toby's soft snuffle-snores in the dark bedroom and sat up to look at the clock. 6:32. The clock clicked and music started playing softly. Toby snuffled one last time and turned over.

"Hi," said Rith.

"Hey," Toby yawned. "You're awake. You okay?"

Rith flopped back down on the cot, looking up at the dark shadows of dragons on the ceiling. An extra dollop of complexity.

"Yeah," he said. "I am. I want to call my mom."

Toby handed him the phone and he called her cell. She picked up, sounding wide awake. Yes, Emma was fine. They'd be letting her go home today. No, she didn't know what time. Sometime in the afternoon. She'd probably be there when he got home from school or if not then, soon after.

Rith and Toby got ready for school. Liz made eggs for breakfast, and Rith checked his backpack to make sure he had his homework from two days ago. Eric dropped them off and they went into the building, Toby heading up to the third floor and Rith putting his jacket in his locker. The hallways, his locker, his school books. They were solid, real. Maybe forty-two zones of reality away from the blizzard cat-yowling dream world he'd come from.

But the two worlds mixed and mingled all day long. His story had been on the local news. Kids who had never talked to him before came up to him in the hallway to tell him he was cool. Two different teachers read the newspaper article about him out loud. Even some girls talked to him. Maybe they had no idea what had actually happened, but it still felt good. Not evil. Good. They even spelled his name right in the paper. Orithian Haley.

The front door was unlocked and Rith came in from the cold, dumping his back-pack and gym bag in the entryway. Walt's voice came from the dining room to his left.

"No, I can't come in, I told you that. No, not today at all. Listen, Kelly, can't you just figure it out? Okay, okay. Yeah. No, it's all right. Put him on."

Rith took off his boots and poked his head around the corner. Walt was at the big wooden dining room table, papers spread out in front of him, his cell phone headset on.

"Is Emma okay?" asked Rith.

Walt, forehead furrowed, nodded and showed Rith a thumbs-up.

"Kelly, I can't be on the phone all day," he said. "Go find Mike and put him on, or else deal with it yourself."

Rith went into the kitchen and opened cupboards, pulling out cereal and a bowl. Ben began to cry from the nursery.

"Rith, can you get the baby?" asked Walt.

Rith was hungry. He didn't want to get the baby. He poured the cereal and opened the refrigerator. Ben yelled again, louder. Walt caught Rith's eye through the doorway and jerked his head toward the nursery.

By the time Rith got to him, Ben's face was beet red and wet, little fists clenched.

"Yo Ben, quit screaming."

Ben, surprised out of his fury, gave Rith a wide blue look. His breath caught, and more tears ran out of his eyes. His screams lost their power, like an air horn trailing off.

"Come here, baby," said Rith, reaching down for him.

Ben reached his arms out for Rith and threw all the warmth of his weight and body into Rith's chest. Rith almost dropped him.

"My god, you stink!"

Rith had changed a diaper or two but never one that smelled like that. Mom did most everything with the kids. Since Mom wasn't here, Walt was next in line. Rith hustled out to the dining room with Ben, trying not to think about what was squishing around in his arms.

Walt was still on the phone. Rith held Ben out toward him. Walt, very red in the face, waved him away.

"But his diaper . . ." whispered Rith.

"Hang on, Mike," said Walt. He put his hand over the phone and looked at Rith.

"What's the matter?"

"He needs a diaper change," said Rith. "He stinks."

"Well then, go do it. Sorry, Mike, what did you say?"

Ben squawked. He didn't like being held out at arm's length, and he was heavy. He squirmed and kicked, and Rith pulled him back in close. Ben let go with a holler in Rith's ear. Walt flapped his hand again, shoving them away.

Rith headed back to the nursery, fuming. Why should he have to take care of the baby? It wasn't his baby. Nobody even asked him if he wanted another baby around. Besides, he'd already saved one baby. Couldn't Walt take care of his own kids?

He put Ben down on the changing table and backed up so he could get a couple of breaths of good air. What to do? He couldn't just leave him like that. Ben was working himself into a red-faced, screaming frenzy. Rith took a deep breath and stepped in.

The diaper was the nastiest thing he'd ever seen. It looked even worse than it smelled. The mess went beyond Ben's diaper, all the way to his little green socks. Rith, breathing through his mouth and turning his head aside every few seconds, managed to mop up most of it, using half the box of wipes on the changing table. He threw everything in the plastic-lined garbage pail. Surely no one would try to wash those clothes. Just looking at them made him gag.

Once he was free of the diaper, Ben squawked and waved his fists and peed all over himself and the changing table. Rith managed to strap a new diaper on him and work some clothes onto the squirmy little body. Mom could give him a bath when she got home and get whatever was left in the cracks.

He hoisted Ben up in his arms again and put him in the mechanical swing by the window. Ben squealed and chewed on his hands, his face back to normal color, looking like a fat little prince again. Walt came up behind him in the doorway.

"Sorry about that, Rith. Everything's going to hell at work. You'd think a guy could miss a day now and then without everybody falling apart. Did you have any trouble?"

Rith didn't answer, didn't turn around. Walt didn't care. He just wanted everything his own way. Rith looked at the floor, waiting for Walt to leave so he could go back to his cereal.

Walt cleared his throat. "Listen, Rith," he said. "I want to thank you for saving Emma. She would have died if it wasn't for you. We'd never have found her before morning. I can't think of anything big enough to thank you. But if you think of something, say the word."

"I didn't do it for you," Rith said, turning to face Walt.

One time when Ty was wrestling Rith into the couch cushions, Rith had jerked an elbow and hit Ty right in the mouth. The look that ran across Ty's face—the color, the shock, the start of tears in his eyes—had been like a sped-up cartoon. Then Ty had blinked the water back, touched his swelling lip, grinned, and said, "Wow, good shot, Rithman."

The look that went across Walt's face was the same. Exactly the same. But he didn't say anything about a good shot. He stepped around Rith and squatted in front of the swing.

"Hey Benji boy, want to come and do some paperwork with Daddy?"

Walt lifted Ben from the swing and took him out of the room without looking at Rith. He was hurt. Rith had hurt Walt. He didn't even know Walt could be hurt.

Be angry but sin not. As loud in his head as if Bible Man were sitting right there on the changing table saying it. But he wasn't there. No one was. Rith stood alone in the nursery, surrounded by the leftover smell of Ben's stinky diaper.

He slipped out of the nursery, avoiding Walt and Ben. He left the bowl of cereal on the counter and hustled up the stairs to his room, closing the door behind him. Walt didn't care what anyone else said or thought. He just bossed everyone around and did what he wanted. But that look on his face—he didn't really think Rith went out in the storm for him, did he? Bible Man said not to hide hatred with lying lips. Rith could have said, *Sure Walt, glad to help you out,* but that would have been a big lie.

Rith threw himself down on his bed. It would help if Bible Man would explain something every now and then instead of just dumping Bible words on him and then taking off again. So what if he hated Walt, who wouldn't? Instead of a cool dad like Eric, he had dumb old Walt giving him orders and threatening to tell him a thing or two.

Rith folded his hands behind his head. The sun was low

in the sky, slanting golden light in the window. On his windowsill was the jar where he kept spare change, and the last rays of the sun streamed through it, lighting it up. It was full of pennies, quarters, dimes. And nickels.

Rith fished a nickel out of the jar. He held it up to the light. *E pluribus unum.* Monticello. Five cents. He turned it over and looked at the square-jawed profile of Thomas Jefferson. For one nickel. His mind went quiet, all of the fuming and arguing about Walt silenced. One nickel. Rith moved like someone else was running the controls, out the door and down the stairs.

Rith paused on the carpeted landing, then descended slowly. One step at a time. The stairs were carpeted but Rith felt like he was walking down a spiral. Toward something. The feeling walked with him through the kitchen and into the doorway of the dining room.

"Hey Walt," he said.

Walt sat at the foot of the table with his back to the bay window, calculator and papers spread on the smooth dark wood in front of him. Ben lay on the floor, sucking his fist.

"What?" Walt asked without looking up.

"I thought of how you can thank me for saving Emma."

The nickel was warm and smooth in his palm.

"How?" said Walt, continuing to write on the paper in front of him.

"One time, you said for a nickel you'd tell me a thing or two. Well, here's a nickel."

Cli-click. Rith set the nickel on the table. It lay alone, a spot of perfectly round silver on the expanse of dark polished wood. Walt looked at the nickel. Up at Rith. Back at the nickel.

"Which thing or two did you want to know?" asked Walt, setting down his pen.

"The thing or two Mom won't let you tell me."

Walt looked at the nickel for a long time. The flush moved across his face like paint spilling upwards. Rith felt the heat rise in his own face and he swallowed hard. Walt looked at Rith again, and for the first time since that Super Bowl day at Uncle Don's, Rith didn't look away. He didn't roll his eyes or glance sideways. He stood solid, his feet spread and his arms folded over his chest, and met Walt eye to eye.

"Okay," said Walt, nodding. "Sit down there, I've got something to show you."

He pushed his chair back and got up, stepping over Ben and leaving the room. Rith stood where he was, a hard burning behind his eyes. Even with all that had happened, he'd managed to keep thinking it was a dream or a story—Bible Man, the fights between Mom and Walt, the blizzard . . . just some twist of his imagination, not reality.

Walt came through the doorway with a book in his hand and set it on the table in front of Rith. It was a battered Bible. Rith stepped forward and touched it. The cover was dirty white, worn down to thread. The binding was broken, flapping loose at the bottom. He ran his fingertips lightly over the bumpy surface of the cover.

"That's yours," said Walt.

"Mine?" Rith drew his hand away.

Walt returned to his chair and sat back, folding his arms and crossing an ankle over his knee.

"Ga," said Ben from the floor.

"You should really sit down for this," Walt said.

Rith shook his head and stood solid, forcing himself not to look away. If Walt was going to lie to him now, he wanted to know it.

"I'm going to tell you the truth because you asked me and because it's wrong not to tell you. And because . . ."

He looked down at the table. Walt. Walt looked down.

"I don't think your mom ever will. And she's not going to like it that I do."

Rith's pulse pounded so hard, he almost swayed back and forth from the force of it.

"It's gonna be a bit of a rough ride, okay?" said Walt. "So grab hold."

When you walk through the fire, I will be with you. The thought was in Rith's head as loudly as if someone had shouted it. He squeezed his fists tight in his pockets.

"Your dad didn't die ten years ago," said Walt. "He died

a few weeks ago. That was his Bible."

The words were sounds, bombs of sound dropping around Rith. He heard them, he understood the meaning, but they were far away. Like a TV show, like a movie, like a video game, like a . . .

"He was in prison," said Walt. "In Florida. He told your mom to tell you he was dead. And she did. But he wasn't."

Poof. Like one of those mushroom clouds from a long, long way away. And another one. The distant explosion, the rise of the pattern of dirt and dust, but it was so far away. Way down there at the end of the table.

"I'm sorry. That's gotta be rough to hear. But that Bible there, it's yours. The prison sent it, he wanted you to have it. I guess he changed his mind about you knowing. Kinda seems like the weak way out to me, to wait until he's dead and then slam you with it, but—"

Rith narrowed his eyes. Walt put up both hands.

"I know. I know. Don't say anything bad about the dad. But look, Rith, I'm just trying to say I think you got a raw deal. All the way around. None of it's fair to you, not even me telling you this now. It's not like I don't know what you think of me, I'm the last guy you want to hear this stuff from."

Rith looked down at the Bible.

And the rivers, they shall not overflow you.

"Ba!" yelled Ben from the floor. "A habada!"

"Got a lot for that nickel, didn't you?" said Walt as he leaned over to pick Ben up.

His voice was softer than Rith had ever heard it. The nickel lay on the dark polished wood. Rith fixed his eyes on the silver circle, the one clearly outlined thing in the fog.

Rith and Walt both jumped at the sound of the garage door. Their eyes met for a split second, and then Rith turned toward the rear entryway. The door opened, coats rustled, and boots came off. Emma's voice. Mom's voice. Rith, Walt, Ben, the nickel, and the Bible were all on pause, a frozen snapshot.

Mom came through the kitchen and into the dining room with Emma in her arms. She looked from one end of the table to the other. She looked at the Bible. She closed her eyes in a long blink, then looked at Walt.

"What have you done?"

Rith's heart thudded. Lies. All lies. Everything.

"Daddy!" yelled Emma, struggling to get down.

Walt set Ben on the floor and scooped Emma up as she ran to him. She threw her arms around his neck.

"Rith . . ." said Mom.

Rith picked up the Bible, holding it carefully in both hands. It was his. Walt said so. He turned, leaving the nickel on the table. Past Mom and through the kitchen, where his bowl of cereal still sat on the counter. Up the carpeted stairs. Into his room. Shut the door behind him.

All lies.

He set the Bible on his desk. The street outside, the snow piles, the garbage cans on the curb, the big houses. All lies. Even back at their old house, B.W., back in his purple bedroom. Lies there too. Everything.

A knock on the door.

Lies.

"Rith, I'm coming in."

He folded his arms across his chest, staring out at the bare branches, at the clear sky fading to a darker gray, puffs of purple on the western horizon. It held no warmth. The door opened behind him and the overhead light came on.

"Rith, give me a chance to explain."

"Why?" he said, his voice as cold coming out of him as the wind that rattled the twigs on the trees.

The bedroom door closed. He hoped she wouldn't come any closer. If she touched him, he might hit her. He held his arms tight against his chest.

"I didn't want it to happen like this," she said. "I'm so mad at Walt. He knew I didn't want him to tell you."

Rith turned to face her. She slid down the wall, sinking to sit on the floor with her hands clasped around her knees. For once in his life he felt tall, righteous. He was right and she was wrong, everyone was wrong.

"The truth? You didn't want him to tell me the truth? Well guess what, I asked him to."

He narrowed his eyes, shooting the cold wind out at her.

"I knew you were lying to me about something. I could feel it. What about all that church stuff, huh? It's fake. A bunch of big fat lies. You're probably getting ready to tell me some other lie right now."

The way she sat there looking up at him made him even madder. A fire flared in his chest and he stepped closer.

"How can I ever believe what you say? What am I supposed to do, ask Walt?"

The flames leapt higher and Rith was afraid of himself, afraid of what he might do. He clenched his fists, breathing hard.

"It's my *dad* we're talking about. *Mine. My* dad, not Walt's."

Mom crumpled, her face in her hands. He raged on, cold wind whipping up hot flame.

"What kind of mother are you, anyway?"

He wanted her to stand up and give him something to fight with, somewhere to go with all of the feeling surging through his body.

"I'm sorry," she said, looking up at him, her face red and blotchy. "I'm so sorry."

"That's not good enough!" he yelled, stomping. "So what if you're sorry! I had a dad! I don't care if he was in prison, I could've written letters to him, I could have gone to visit him. I could have, I don't know, asked him stuff. Found out about my name. How could you do that to me? Do you hate me?"

He stood swaying, the question dangling in the air between them. Mom closed her eyes, bit her lower lip. Then she pushed herself up off the floor and stepped close to Rith.

"I do not hate you," she said, her voice shaking but fierce. "You are my son and I love you."

"You're just saying that." He stood his ground. "You have to but you don't mean it. You love Ben and Emma more. You think I don't know that? You think I'm stupid?

You'd get rid of me in a second if you could."

Rith smacked her hard with his words, watched them land on her face like a handprint slap. Her eyes filled and his did too, dousing the fire of his rage. He folded into his desk chair, elbows on his knees and head down.

"Rith," Mom said, her voice low. "Orithian James Haley. Listen to me. I've been afraid of this day for years. And you know what?"

Rith kept his eyes fixed on the blue carpet.

"I'm relieved. I'm actually relieved. Isn't that funny?"

He shook his head, wiping his nose on the back of his hand.

"No, I guess it's not funny to you. Oh, Rith. Will you just look at me?"

She moved around to sit cross-legged in front of him on the floor and put her hands on his ankles.

"Then I'll sit here so I can look at you," she said. "Because I love you. Because you're my boy."

He shook his head again, swallowing back the choky feeling in his throat.

"Yes, you are. Like it or not, you're mine. Your father quit on you, Rith. He was so ashamed, he didn't want you to know him. He quit. I didn't quit. I'm still here."

He swallowed again, swallowed hard. "Well whoopee for you," he said.

"Yes," she said. "Whoopee for me. It was hard, Rith! How was I supposed to tell you that your dad was alive but wouldn't write you a lousy letter? When you were four? Six? I know you don't like Walt, but I'll tell you one thing. He would never do that. Even if he was in prison, he wouldn't do that because he's not a liar. And he doesn't like that I am. So chew on that next time you want to roll your eyes over Walt."

Rith heard her breath shake on the way in, but it was steady coming out.

"What did he do?" asked Rith. "My dad. What did he do?"

"Does it matter?" she asked.

"Yes."

He finally lifted his head and met her eyes. She took a huge breath, sucking up all the air in the room.

"Driving while intoxicated. Head-on collision. Four counts of manslaughter. Possession of cocaine."

Each word hit Rith like a blow, a sweep of shame. He'd been so stupid.

"He was running drugs from Florida," Mom said.

"Why?"

Why why why? The question stomped around in Rith's head. Finally, she spoke.

"You know the part of your brain that stops you in the middle sometimes and tells you that what you're doing might not be a good idea?"

Rith nodded.

"I think that part was broken in your dad. Or maybe he never had it to start with. He wasn't a bad guy, Rith. He wasn't mean, he'd never hurt anyone on purpose."

"He killed four people?"

"In the car accident. He never meant to kill anyone. I'm

sure he wanted to make money to buy things for us. He was crazy about you, I never saw a man prouder of a baby."

"Then why didn't he care what happened to me?"

Mom sighed. Rith could feel truth circling the room. There was a smell to it, the smell of a wood fire.

"Your dad was good at dreams," said Mom. "Not reality. He couldn't have stood it, to have you look at him and think he was anything other than the greatest man in the world."

Emma and Ben looked at Walt like that while Rith stood off to the side and sneered, knowing they were wrong, knowing they were just babies who didn't know what a loser Walt was. Now he could see Walt, looking at Rith who thought his dad was so great, knowing what a loser his dad was. No wonder Walt kept saying that thing about him not facing reality.

"Is Emma really okay?" Rith asked.

Mom nodded.

"She's going to be fine. A little bit of frostbite on her cheek and her left ear, but by the time we left the hospital it was hard to keep her in bed."

"I think I want to be alone now," Rith said.

"Are you sure?" Mom asked.

She reached to touch his cheek but he moved back. Her hand hovered in midair for a moment and then dropped to her side.

"Wait," Rith said while the truth was still in the room. "Is this it? Is this my last chance? Or can I ask you more questions later?"

"Oh Rith. I don't want to drag this out forever."

His mouth dropped open. He couldn't believe she'd said that.

"You're right," she said, quickly. "You're right, of course you can ask more later and I'll try." The last word broke. She swallowed, then went on, her voice high and shaking. "I'll try to tell you. It hurts me too, Rith. Don't forget, I loved him."

She reached out for the Kleenex box on Rith's nightstand and wiped her face and blew her nose.

"But I'll try," she said. "I will."

"And that," Rith pointed to the Bible on his desk. "I get to keep that? Walt said it's mine."

Mom nodded, backing toward the door. She was only barely holding herself together. Any minute now that trickle of tears was going to start surging over the banks and flood everything in sight. He didn't want to see it.

Rith picked up the Bible on his desk. It wasn't the same as Bible Man's. His was black and much bigger. He settled against the headboard of his bed and opened the book. *The Holy Bible Presented To: Kyle James Haley by Aunt Marna, 1981.*

He fanned the pages with his thumb, feeling the softness of the old paper. The pages were edged with a gold color gone dull yellow, spotted and thin. He flipped more slowly through the pages and caught a glimpse of an ink marking. An underlined passage.

Give instruction to a wise man and he will be still wiser. Rith glanced at the top of the page. Proverbs. Quickly, he flipped to Proverbs 26:11. *Like a dog that returns to his vomit is a fool that repeats his folly.* It was underlined too.

Whoa. He flipped pages, searching for underlinings. There were lots. Some that Bible Man had said, others that he hadn't. So was Bible Man . . . ?

No. Bible Man was old. White-haired. He couldn't be.

Now Rith turned pages one at a time, scanning for every mark. His dad, Kyle Haley, had made those. He'd held this very same book in his hands, read it, and underlined things. Maybe Bible Man talked to him too. Maybe Bible Man was a messenger, some kind of angel.

More pages. More underlinings. *A man of quick temper acts foolishly, but a man of discretion is patient.* Rith shook his head and paged through, looking. He wanted something special, something written just for him.

The heart is deceitful above all things, and desperately corrupt.

No, that was no help.

Who has put wisdom in the clouds or given understanding to the mists?

Blah blah, no good.

A wise son hears his father's instruction.

Rith threw the Bible across the room and it lay there crumpled against the wall, its binding hanging loose.

"Get real," he said, glaring at it.

His father was a liar and a murderer and a drug dealer. And dead.

Hunger finally drove him out of his room around eight and he stomped down looking for a fight. A light was on in the kitchen, spilling shadows into the living room, where Mom sat on the couch staring into the darkness.

"Where is everyone?" he asked as he hit the bottom stair.

"Walt went to Don's," said Mom. "He took Ben and Emma with him."

"Why?"

"To give us some time to work this thing through. How are you?" she asked the dark TV screen, not even looking at him.

"Fine," he said. "I'm just getting a sandwich."

He stepped into the light of the kitchen and her voice followed him.

"Rith. What can I do to make this right? Anything?"

He opened the cupboard, pulled out the peanut butter, and banged the door shut.

"You're stuck with me, you know," she said, raising her voice. "I'm the only mother you're ever going to have."

He pulled out a couple of slices of bread and jerked the silverware drawer open. When he turned around, Mom was leaning in the doorway. The circles under her eyes were darker than ever. Even her hair looked tired.

"Is there anything else you want to ask?" she said.

"Why bother?" he said to the refrigerator as he opened it. "You'll just lie."

He poured himself a glass of milk and walked by her. She put a hand on his shoulder as he passed and he stopped. Not jerking away but not looking at her, not giving an inch.

"Somehow, Rith, you and I are going to have to find a way."

"Well let me know when you find it." He dipped his shoulder, moving out from beneath her hand. "I'm going to bed."

Mom knocked on his door the next morning, saying, "Rith, are you awake?" She came in and sat on the edge of his bed.

"Rith," she said, putting a hand on his forehead and smoothing his hair back. She hadn't done that in ages. He didn't pull away.

"How are you this morning? Still mad?"

He nodded.

"You're a harsh judge and I'm a coward. It's a bad mix."

She brought her hand down on his cheek, cool and soft. Like she used to do B.W.

"I promise," she said. "I won't lie to you again."

He narrowed his eyes and she tapped his hot cheek with a forefinger.

"I know what you're thinking," she said. "But you're wrong. Come down and have some pancakes."

She left him to get up and get ready for school. As he got dressed, he noticed the Bible lying in a heap where he'd thrown it. It looked twisted and uncomfortable.

"All right, all right," he said, picking it up.

He put it on his desk, smoothed down the creased pages, and closed the cover.

"Rith! Breakfast is ready."

He grabbed his backpack and followed the smell of sausage downstairs. Mom set a plate in front of him.

"I'm trying to bribe you with food," she said. "Is it working?"

He shook his head.

"What will work?"

"You know that thing you say about let's not think about the past? Our good lives now and all that? Don't ever say that again."

"Okay," she agreed. "I won't ever say that again."

Rith poured syrup on the pancakes and spread it around in the melting butter with the back of his fork.

"Did you know Dad had that Bible?" he asked.

"His aunt gave it to him," she said, nodding. "He left it in the dresser drawer. The prison chaplain sent a post-card a few years ago asking for it."

"And they sent it back to you when he died?" Rith asked, cramming sausage in his mouth.

"Yes. Your dad wanted you to have it."

"So were you ever going to give it to me?"

He searched her eyes on this one, daring her to lie to him.

"I don't know. I told myself I would, but Rith, now you know. I'm a coward. I hope I would have someday when the time was right. I didn't want you to find out the way you did."

"Walt told me the truth," said Rith, stomping on the word *truth*.

"That's new." Mom smiled. "You sticking up for Walt."

"I'm not sticking up for him," said Rith, clattering the fork down on the empty plate. "I'm telling the truth. When's he coming back, anyway?"

Mom flinched from the question. He didn't actually see her move, but he felt it. "What's going on?" he asked.

"Do you want some more pancakes?" she asked, pushing away from the table.

"So much for telling me the truth," he said.

He stared out at the patio, slouched down with his arms across his chest. An upside-down mountain range of icicles hung from the roof.

"Rith," she said, coming back to the table with three pancakes on the spatula. "Some things aren't your business."

"Fine, then tell me this," he said, reaching for the butter. "Did Walt really go to give us time alone? Or was it because you guys are fighting?"

"Both," she said.

"What are you fighting about? Me?"

"That's my business."

She left Rith alone in the kitchen with his pancakes. He ate them slowly, sopping up the last bits of syrup on the plate. She'd made them just the way he liked, thick and soft in the middle. Walt liked thin ones. That's how she usually made them.

Mom came back in with an envelope and sat across from him, pulling pictures out of it. She laid three snapshots on the table in front of Rith's plate.

"That's your dad and me the year we met," she said. "And that's him the first Christmas we moved in together. And that," she said, pointing to a picture of a toddler sitting on a man's shoulders, "is you. Do you recognize that rock?"

"Yeah, that's Mount Rock. Behind our old house."

"Right. He named it that and took you out to climb on it all the time. I was sure you'd fall off but you never did."

"Why didn't you show me these before?" asked Rith, holding the one of himself up close. A cap shadowed his father's face, but his own was wide open in the sun with a big baby smile, just like the ones he saw all the time on Ben and Emma.

"I should have. I just . . . every time I said anything about your dad, you asked questions and then I got caught up trying to remember what I'd said last time and . . . it was easier not to."

Rith set the pictures down and leaned back, crossing his arms. Mom took his plate to the sink and rinsed it and he pulled the pictures closer. The goofy one of the two of them making faces in a photo booth. The one of his dad throwing a surprised look over his shoulder with the Christmas tree behind him. And the one of Rith laughing in the sunshine.

In that one, Rith could feel the warmth of Mount Rock. He remembered climbing it with his friend Sam after school, back when he was little. Remembered Mom bringing out peanut butter sandwiches and handing them up to the top of the mountain.

He rearranged the pictures, stacking them in a vertical row and then spreading them out. Mom sat down at the table and reached both hands across, palms up. She waggled her fingers. Calling him. When he didn't move, she reached over and took his hand, sandwiching it in hers. He didn't pull away.

"You look so much like your father," she said. "More all the time."

It was true. He looked like the man in the pictures. Especially the surprised-looking one. A morph of his own face.

The bus honked outside and they both ignored it. Mom drove him to school.

When Rith opened the front door after school, Emma came flying into him and wrapped herself around his leg.

"Rit!" she yelled.

"Hey Emma."

He kicked off his boots and went over to flop on the couch. It had been a long day, with his mind on everything but school. He'd managed to avoid Toby all day because he had no idea what to say to him. About anything.

Emma came to stand by Rith's head, patting him.

"I'm not a dang dog, Emma. Stop patting me."

She patted him some more and he yelled "Woof!" in her face.

She jerked away in surprise, then laughed and barked back, "Woof," in her little baby voice.

"Meow?" asked Rith, watching her closely.

"Meow!" she yelled, laughing.

Who could tell the difference? She'd been just as happy about woof.

Walt still wasn't home. He'd dropped the babies off in the morning but he was staying at Uncle Don's again. Mom and Rith walked carefully on their new ground, Rith asking questions and Mom answering. He watched her when she talked, looking for lies. Mom was distracted by the babies and they were both tired, but he learned more in one evening than he'd known his whole life.

His dad had always been short, grew to five foot nine and stopped. He hated math. Loved skateboarding and rock and roll, and did very funny imitations of people. He hadn't known his father. His mother was killed in a boating accident when he was seven, and he'd been raised by the great-aunt who gave him the Bible. For Rith, the information was like a huge meal after years of starvation.

Before he went to sleep that night, he tucked the pictures of his dad in between the thin pages of the Bible. The photo booth one on the page about lying lips. The Christmas tree one by the dog vomit verse. And the one of him and his dad in Isaiah, where it said, *I have called you by name, you are mine.*

The cat sounded very far away. Rith tried to move toward the constant, insistent meowing, but he couldn't quite pull himself out of sleep. He went back under. When he woke, it was daylight.

"I missed it," he said. "They were here, and I missed it."

He threw himself back on his pillow. Tears came up in his eyes and he didn't try to stop them. Bright sun flooded the room and Rith hated it. He wanted darkness. He wanted Bible Man.

"Meow."

Rith heard it distinctly. He sat straight up and cocked his head.

"Meow."

Rith wiped his eyes, scrambled out of bed, and yanked his door open. Laughter came from downstairs, followed by the cat's agreeable little squeaky noise. Rith jerked some clothes on and ran to the top of the stairs. Wide, no-color carpeting. No wood, no spiral.

"Meep," followed by more voices and laughter.

Rith rushed down the stairs and into the kitchen. A small gray cat leapt away from the crumpled ball of paper in the middle of the floor and froze in a crouch. The yellow eyes held Rith still in the doorway. The gray tail twitched.

"Kitty!" yelled Emma, squirming to get off of Walt's lap.

Rith and the cat stared at each other. Same yellow eyes. Narrow body. Long white eyebrow hair. No collar. Same cat. It had to be the same cat.

Rith squatted down and held his hand out. The cat stretched her neck to sniff his fingers. Rith edged closer, reaching. She took a step forward and leaned into his hand.

"See, Emma?" said Mom. "See how Rith is slow and gentle with the kitty?"

Rith sat cross-legged on the floor.

"Where did it come from?" he asked, barely trusting his voice.

"We don't know," said Walt. "I pulled up around seven this morning and she was sitting on the front porch like she owned the place. She seemed hungry so I let her in and gave her some half and half."

"Emma kitty," said Emma, and followed up with a long string of babble, punctuated with an occasional "kitty." She squirmed free from Walt's grasp.

"Wait," Walt said. "Let Rith show you how to pet the kitty."

Rith darted a quick glance at Walt. He hadn't seen him

since the nickel day. The cat dodged sideways as Emma ran across the kitchen and threw her arms around Rith's neck, almost knocking him over.

"Whoa, Emma. Hang on."

Rith reached up, releasing his head from her squeeze, and turned her to sit on his lap. She lunged for the cat, but he stopped her and gently pulled her back. He put his cheek up against her soft baby face. The cat moved over to where the sun streamed in the sliding glass door, baking heat into the earth-colored tiles. She set about the business of cleaning her face and whiskers.

"Do you like the kitty?" Rith whispered in Emma's ear.

Emma squirmed around and stood so she was nose-to-nose with Rith. She talked very earnestly, a long string of consonants and vowels mixed with "kitty" and "Rit" and "Emma." Rith strained to understand, tried to find words in the puzzle, but he couldn't.

"She's sure telling you a story or two about that cat," said Mom.

Rith glanced at Mom. Her face showed nothing. Nothing about Emma and the cat, or the fight with Walt or anything else. The cat continued on its serious business, three licks to the paw and a rub across the ear, over and over. Emma reached out again, but Rith wrapped his arms around her body and held her hands in.

"Shhhh, easy," he said. "Easy with the kitty."

He got up on his knees and together they crawled toward the cat. The cat stopped grooming and watched out of the corner of her eye. Rith took Emma's sticky hand in his and reached it out. The cat sniffed and then licked Emma's finger. Emma tensed but didn't move.

"Shhh," said Rith, imagining how that rough tongue felt on Emma's fingertip. "Look, the kitty likes you."

Emma quivered, then jumped and let loose with a big giggle. The cat leapt back, and Emma ran over and climbed up on Walt's knee, pointing at the cat and laughing, a fresh river of happy baby noise dancing through the kitchen with the morning sunbeams. The cat edged over to Rith, purring. She arched into his touch as his hand ran along the length of her spine, drawing her tail across his palm.

"Can we keep her?" he asked.

"She must belong to someone," said Mom. "She doesn't look like a stray."

"She doesn't have a collar," said Rith.

"You're right," said Walt. "I say we let her stay. If nobody claims her, we adopt her."

Rith looked up in time to see Mom do an eye-message thing with Walt. Then she held out her hand for Emma.

"Come on, Emma," she said. "Come help Mama get Ben dressed."

Rith's stomach flipped. Now he was alone in the kitchen with Walt. The cat sprawled on the floor beside him and he continued to focus on the gray fur, the softness of it. Walt cleared his throat and Rith glanced up. Walt's face was so red, Rith thought liquid color might come out of his pores and run down his cheeks.

"Rith," Walt said. He cleared his throat and started

again. "Rith, now that the truth is on the table, I'm hoping you and I can straighten some things out."

A shiver of nerves ran through Rith. He hand shook slightly as he ran it across the cat's side. The fine hairs drifted up with static electricity.

"First thing, this is for you." Walt reached into his pocket and held a nickel out on his palm. "It's the same one," he said. "You shouldn't have had to pay for that."

Rith looked at the nickel, at Walt's outstretched hand. He got up on one knee, leaned forward, and took it.

"I can't ever be your father, I know that. And I gotta hand it to you. When I told you about him the other day, you took it on the chin. I respect that."

Rith went back to petting the cat. She started up a soft purring.

"The thing is, I don't really get you. You're a different kind of kid than I was, different than Ty. There's nothing wrong with it, I just don't know what to do with you."

Silence settled across the kitchen as Walt waited for a response. Rith stroked the cat, head to tail. Walt took a big breath and blew it out, long.

"Don says I have to put myself in your shoes. He said I should talk to you about that time I dragged you out of their house. You remember that time?"

Rith remembered, all right. The cat licked her paw, then rubbed her face. Lick, lick, lick, rub. Like she hadn't done a good enough job the first time.

"I told him I didn't have any choice," said Walt. "I said you'd never respect me if I let you walk all over me. But

I'm thinking that didn't make you respect me any."

Was it the same cat? It had to be, but how could it be? The cat moved from face-washing to body-licking, drawing its head back to clean its shoulder. Lick, lick, lick, in the silent space between Walt's words.

"So I'm sorry about that. That was a mistake. Maybe we can start this whole thing over. What do you say?"

The words circled around Rith in the quiet kitchen. Start over. What did that mean?

The cat sat up and shuddered. She moved away from Rith and writhed like she was trying to turn herself inside out. She heaved and showed her entire mouth full of sharp little teeth, made a retching hacking noise that went right to the back of Rith's throat, and brought up something nasty and slimy. She shook her head, licked her lips, and backed away.

Rith gag-coughed and Walt laughed out loud as the cat strolled out of the kitchen, leaving a pile of yellow slimy liquid on the sunny spot of tile.

"Well, I guess we know what the cat thinks of my little speech," Walt said. "And I practiced it and everything."

Rith coughed again, running a hand over his eyes. They had watered up when he gagged.

"You're not going to puke too, are you?" asked Walt.

"No," said Rith. "I didn't think your speech was *that* bad."

"Jane," hollered Walt. "Jane, the cat just puked out here in the kitchen."

Rith scrambled to his feet, put his hands in his pockets,

and waited for Mom to come and figure out what to do.

"Well, clean it up then," came Mom's voice from the bedroom.

Rith went to the sink, pulled off a long string of paper towels, and wadded them up. He walked over to the pile of kitty puke, looked down at the mess, and then handed the paper towels to Walt. Walt looked at him and Rith looked back and they held each other like that, neither of them moving. The refrigerator hummed.

"For me, huh?"

Rith nodded.

"Thanks a bunch," said Walt, taking them.

He kept his eyes on Rith, giving a half twist of a smile.

"You're welcome," said Rith. He didn't exactly smile but he did tighten one cheek, lifting the corner of his mouth.

"It's the first thing you ever gave me," Walt said, kneeling down to clean up the mess. "And I appreciate it."

Rith spent a lot of time that Saturday in his room with the Bible, looking for marked passages and reading them. Some of the markings were in pencil, some in blue pen and some in black. Dad's markings, all in the Old Testament. Maybe he started reading at the beginning and that's as far as he got.

Water dripped from the icicles all day. The cold snap was over and winter was starting to lose her grip. Like that blizzard had been her last hurrah. Rith called Toby that evening.

"Hey, you coming to church tomorrow?"

"No, I have to go to my uncle's. Are you okay? I e-mailed you a bunch of times. I thought maybe you were mad or something."

"Sorry. Lots going on here. I've got a bunch of stuff to tell you. Can you come over after your uncle's? You can go to school with me on the bus Monday morning."

Toby set the phone down and Rith could hear him

yelling down the stairs.

"No," he said, picking up the phone again. "We won't be back until too late. How about sometime during the week? After confirmation, maybe? I'm dying to see the stairs. Even if they just stay carpet."

"I gotta ask," said Rith. "I'll let you know."

Toby would go wild when he saw the cat. Rith went back to the Bible, reading the underlined stuff more slowly, thinking about it.

Behold, thou desirest truth in the inward being; therefore teach me wisdom in my secret heart. Psalms 51:6.

You shall not steal, nor deal falsely, nor lie to one another. Leviticus 19:11.

Truthful lips endure for ever; but a lying tongue is but for a moment. Proverbs 12:19.

Looked like Dad had gone through and underlined everything with the word "truth" in it. So was he a liar? Or was he like Rith and just didn't know what reality was? But then Eric said Rith had a pretty good grip on reality. Which was it?

Rith pulled the dictionary off his bookshelf. *Reality. A person, entity or event that is actual. That which exists objectively and in fact.* Rith looked over at the cat, curled up asleep on his pillow. The cat was actual. It existed objectively and in fact. Even Walt could see it. But had it existed objectively and in fact before? And if the cat existed objectively and in fact, did Bible Man? Was he going to show up at the door tomorrow morning and come in for breakfast?

Truth. Conformity to knowledge, fact, actuality or logic. Fidelity to an original or standard. Reality; actuality. Sincerity; integrity; honesty.

Honesty? Truth? Logic? He closed the dictionary and lay back on his bed, wishing someone could help him sort it out. He didn't even know how to tell Toby about his dad. He got up and stood in front of the mirror, testing out loud.

He tilted his head back, hands in his pockets, and said, "Yeah, my dad was a drug runner. He got busted and did time."

Then he opened his eyes wide and said, "My dad made some mistakes—got himself into a lot of trouble."

Arms folded across his chest. "He was a loser. I never knew him."

The last one tasted bad in his mouth. He tried another one.

"My dad was big on the Bible. I guess he must have got religion in jail."

All truth. All reality. All different.

The cat squeaked from Rith's bed. She sat up, yawning and curling her tail around her body.

"Hey," said Rith.

She fixed her large yellow eyes on him.

"So what's the deal? Are you real or not? You look real."

Rith sat on the bed next to her and opened the Bible on his lap.

"Do you want to put a paw on here and show me where to read?"

Her purring engine started up, revving up and down with her breath. He reached a hand out and she rubbed her head into his palm, purring louder.

"Where'd Bible Man go?" he asked, rubbing the base of her ear. "Isn't he looking for you?"

The cat turned toward the door, ears pricked. Seconds later, Mom knocked and stepped in.

"Oh, the cat's up here—hiding out from Emma's love, I guess."

She sat down on the other side of the cat and traced a finger back from the tip of its nose between the soft triangle ears.

"She's pretty, isn't she?"

Rith nodded.

"Mom, there's stuff underlined in this Bible," he said. "Did you know that?"

"No, I didn't look at it. What kind of stuff?"

"All kinds. Lots about truth."

Purrpurrpurr.

"Mom, was Dad a liar?"

Mom drew her heels up on the bed frame and propped her elbows on her knees. She leaned forward, holding her chin in her hands.

"Not really a liar most of the time," she said. "He just . . . well, he'd think things and make them seem almost real. Like the house he was going to build, he talked about it so many times I could see it myself, could move from room to room in it. Maybe way inside I knew it was never going to happen but he was so . . ."

Purrpurrpurr.

"So what?" asked Rith.

"I don't know, so sure, so excited, so . . . when you saw him smile, when you saw how excited he'd get over something, you wanted to believe it. So you would. Even though you knew it was just a dream."

"Like my name? You think he made it up and then said it was something Greek and you wanted to believe it?"

"Maybe like that," said Mom. "I went to the library and looked, I even asked the librarian but she couldn't find anything either. Whatever it was, it was real to him and that's what counted. It's a beautiful name and it suits you perfectly."

"Yeah," said Rith. "Yeah, I like it. I just wondered. Would you say Dad didn't know what reality was?"

"No," said Mom. "I think he knew. Because when I pushed him sometimes, he knew. But I think he thought it was . . . bendable. If he wanted something bad enough, he could make it be just by having it in his head."

"Toby can't come tomorrow," said Rith, after a pause. "How about after confirmation on Wednesday?"

"A school night?"

"Come on Mom. Sunday's a school night too. And I promise we won't stay up too late and we'll do our homework right away."

"All right then. If you promise. He seems like a good friend. Have you told him any of this?"

"Not yet," said Rith. "But I'm going to."

Mom stood up, looking out the window.

"Mom?"

"Yes, Rith."

"Seems like things are okay between you and Walt?"

"Yes, they are. Time for bed now."

"Mom?"

"What?"

"Are you really done lying to me?"

She turned to face him.

"I sure hope so," she said.

Sunday morning, Rith watched the adults in church. This whole pack of people came every week but he couldn't figure out why. He started off listening hard, wondering if maybe he'd been missing something all this time. But his mind couldn't get hold of anything; it slipped off the Bible verses like they were coated with Vaseline. The Sunday stupor settled over him. Sit, stand, sing, sit, stand, pray, sit, sing.

When Bible Man talked, the Bible meant something. During the sermon, Rith leaned forward to look at the people in the pew across the aisle. Did they understand what was going on? A man looked at his watch. The woman in front of Rith nudged her husband and he jerked awake. Rith could almost see a sleepy gas wafting down the aisles and drugging people. He tried holding his breath to see if that helped. It didn't work. The gas still soaked in through his skin, shutting his brain down. Just the opposite of Bible Man. If the truth was here, Rith couldn't smell it.

On the bus on the way home from school Wednesday, Rith filled Toby in on everything but the cat. He saved that for a surprise.

"Man, that is so weird about the Bible," Toby said as they stepped onto the front porch. "That your dad marked the same things Bible Man said. Do you think Bible Man showed up in his prison cell?"

"I don't know, maybe," said Rith, opening the door. "It's hard for me to imagine him without the stairs, though. How would my dad get to him?"

Rith and Toby kicked off their shoes at the doorway. The cat stalked around the corner.

"Hi kitty," said Toby. "I didn't know you had a—"

"It's the cat," said Rith, grinning. "It showed up on the doorstep

Toby's eyes popped.

"Rith, is that you?" Mom yelled from the other room.

"*The* cat?" Toby mouthed, not making a sound. "Bible Man's cat?"

"Yeah, it's us," Rith called out while nodding to Toby.

"Hi Toby, glad you're here, you make yourself at home," said Mom, coming out of the babies' room with Ben on her hip. "Rith, you'd better get started with your homework—remember, you promised. I'll have dinner ready in about an hour and we'll leave right after for church."

As soon as Mom went into the kitchen, Toby grabbed Rith's arm and whispered in his ear, "How do you know it's *the* cat? Where'd it come from?"

"Gotta be the same cat, Toby. She's exactly the same. And the way she looks at me sometimes, I can just tell."

"Impossible," said Toby. "Flat-out frickin, full-on impossible."

"I know," said Rith.

It was such a relief to tell Toby everything, the Bible Man piece and the Dad piece and the Bible piece and the cat piece and the Walt piece. Toby wanted to know every detail. He'd actually gone up and down the carpeted steps on his hands and knees, trying to find a switch or a lever or a crack between the worlds. When Mom came out and asked what he was doing, he said he thought maybe he'd lost a nickel and Rith bit his lip to keep from laughing out loud.

Rith hated to stop the conversation and speculation and go to confirmation class. Pastor Paul went on and on about the Last Supper and Communion and Rith tuned him out, thinking about how he'd give anything for one more night with Bible Man. Well, almost anything. Not Dad's Bible, it was there all the time, not just at three in the morning, and it never told him to go up to his house or fell asleep on him. Toby nudged him when it was time to move to small group.

"I don't really get this," Toby said, raising his hand as soon as Mrs. Hughes closed the door. "I mean, I read the stuff but I guess I don't get the point. Why is it supposed to help us now to eat and drink Jesus?"

"Now Toby," said Mrs. Hughes, giving him her best stiff-lipped smile. "We're not 'eating Jesus.' We're saying that He is present with us. When He said to the disciples, 'Take, eat, this is my body,' He was—"

"But it wasn't really his body," said Rith, snapping his head up. "I mean, that wasn't *reality*. Reality, it was just a piece of bread. Like when we get the wafer now, reality, it's just a wafer."

"No, Rith. It's the body of Christ, broken for you. Just like Pastor says."

"No," said Rith, getting more excited. "That isn't reality. Reality, it's a flat wafer thing. Somebody buys it somewhere, right? Like, it gets made in some wafer factory or something, and put in a box, and the church buys them."

Toby nodded. So did Dawn. Monica pinched up her lips and said, "It's a symbol, dummy."

"Right!" said Mrs. Hughes. "Good, Monica. But not just a symbol. It's a special gift from God for forgiveness of our sins. And because Jesus is the Christ, when He said that it was His body and His blood, that's what the wine and bread become. They're sacred."

"So you're saying," Rith said slowly, "that it's true that the wafer is Jesus's body."

"Absolutely," said Mrs. Hughes, smiling harder.

"So maybe truth and reality aren't always exactly the same? Because *reality,* it's a wafer thing from the wafer factory. Like, if you walk up to someone on the street and say what is this, they'll say, oh, it's a wafer thing. They're not going to look at it and say that's Jesus's body."

"Rith, it is *not* the body of Christ if you're walking down the street with it. It's the body of Christ when Pastor gives it to you in church."

"That's what I'm saying! That wafer, it's not the body of Christ objectively and in fact, right? It is if you're in church and Pastor blesses it and all, but objectively and in fact it's a wafer?"

The thin, arched eyebrows came down.

"Rith, I think you're trying to cause trouble more than you're trying to understand. This is a matter of faith. As Christians, we know that it's the body of Christ, broken for us. Now we only have a few minutes left so you can start on your homework, the Two Meals crossword puzzle on page sixteen."

"Wait, can I ask one more thing? I'm really trying to understand. You're saying something can be true even if it isn't reality. Because you know it, even if nobody else does. Right?"

"Rith, the Scripture says it's true, and I know it in my own heart. You can know it too, if you'll just let the Word in and stop arguing. Now get started on your homework, please."

Mrs. Hughes gave him one last plastic smile and turned away. Rith leaned back in his chair, nodding. He didn't need her to say anything else, or Pastor Paul either. He got it.

"You know," Toby said later that night as they lay in sleeping bags on Rith's floor. "I don't know if I'm going to keep coming to church. Hanging up coats was the most fun part."

"Oh no, don't quit on me," said Rith. "I've got another year and a half of confirmation."

"I'll keep coming Wednesdays," said Toby. "That's actually kinda fun. But the getting up early on Sunday morning, not worth it. I mean, Pastor Paul's an okay guy but on Sundays, he's boring. Not like that preacher lady at all. So I want to check out some other churches and a mosque and a temple, and my mom said she'd look up Buddhists in the phone book and see if there's any of those around. Maybe you can come with me. It'd still be church."

"Doubt it," said Rith.

"Well at least ask," said Toby. "Hey, has Walt laid off about the adoption thing?"

"Yup, totally. He's laid off me about everything. I don't know how long that's gonna last though."

"Oof," said Toby as the cat jumped from the bed to his stomach, bouncing from there to the door.

"Can you open the door for her?" asked Rith. "She likes to go down and sleep with Emma."

"Sure." Toby got up on his knees and cracked the door. "Should I leave it open? So we can hear if Bible Man comes?"

"No," said Rith. "He only comes when it's closed and I'm asleep. Anyway, I wonder if the door to outside was open the night Emma got lost because, you know, he left."

"But where would he go? And wouldn't you have seen his footprints? You said you wore his boots, right? Why would he go out in a snowstorm without his boots?"

It wasn't like Rith hadn't thought all of those questions over six or eleven times.

"I think it's one of those truth/reality things," he said. "I know Bible Man was here just the way Mrs. Hughes knows those wafers are Jesus. And in the same way, I'm starting to think maybe he's not coming back."

"You really had her going about those wafers," said Toby. "You sounded just like my dad. I thought her face was going to freeze if she locked that smile on any harder."

"I wasn't trying to make her freeze," said Rith. "I was trying to figure out about Bible Man. Even if I never see him again, when I read those underlined parts in my dad's Bible it's like he's sitting right there. Like he's looking right at me saying, 'A good name is better than precious ointment,' and I'm going, yeah okay, and I get it. Makes a lot more sense to me than eating Jesus. So Bible Man is truth but not reality. I mean, I know I can't show him to you or anyone else. Or even prove that the cat is *the* cat. In reality she could just be a coincidence."

"Huh. Some coincidence."

"Right. And truth, she's the cat."

They lay in the darkness for a while. Then Toby said, "So what do you think he was? For real?"

"In a way," said Rith, "I kinda think he's my dad's Bible. Like he morphed himself into it."

"Well, if he's a Bible now then I guess he won't bring me a snowboard. I'll go back to asking God."

Rith's eyelids started to get heavy. He was almost asleep when the light clicked on.

"What?" he said, sitting up.

"I just thought of something," said Toby. "Your name. Have you Googled it?"

"Yup," said Rith, reaching over to turn off the light. "Orithians are a race from another planet in some Internet game."

"Well, maybe that's it. Let's look."

"No Toby. My dad picked the name thirteen years ago, remember? I don't think they had that kind of game back then, and besides, we didn't even have a computer until we moved in with Walt."

"Oh," said Toby. "Did you check every hit? Second page too?"

"Yeah. Nothing."

A few nights later, Rith woke up at 2:45.
Wide awake. He listened hard. There it was. Another thud, and then a squeak. Bible Man was back!

He opened the door and the cat was there waiting for him. "Is he here?" asked Rith.

One last time, please, just one more. He was scared to look, wanted to look, scared to look. He stopped across from the bathroom, flattened himself against the right-hand wall, and slid to the edge. He spun out to face the stairs.

Carpet.

Rith let all of his hopes out in one big long escaping breath.

"Meep," the cat squeaked, running past his feet to skitter down the stairs. Rith followed, stopping at the landing. The cat stood in middle of the living room, looking up at him.

"Meow."

"You want me to come down there?" he asked.

He could swear she nodded. Even in the semi-dark, even from the landing, the cat pulled him along as clearly as she ever had when Bible Man was there. So he barefooted down the stairs and around the couch. She led him into the glowing nursery lit by two nightlights.

The cat jumped up on Emma's bed, lay down, and curled her tail around her nose. Elmo smiled from one socket and Big Bird glowed yellow from another. The room rocked gently with the sound of the babies' breathing.

Emma rolled onto her side, her hand landing on the gray fur circle of cat. Her curly hair was tousled, and for the first time he noticed Emma's ear. It was small and pointy. Just like his ears. Just like Mom's. Rith's ears were the one thing about him that definitely looked like Mom. Emma had them too.

Rith stepped over to the crib to look at Ben. Ben, with his round little Walt-face and his sturdy mini-Walt body. Sure enough, he had the same small ears, the same shape. A girl at school once told Rith he had foxy ears. He'd never forgotten that. Ben had foxy ears too. Emma and Ben were his sister and brother. That was reality. Objectively and in fact, they were related by blood. Only half blood, but still blood. Looking down at Emma and the cat, Rith reached up and felt his own ear. The brother and sister thing was reality—same mother, same address, same DNA. But the foxy ears, that was truth.

And the cat. She was as much Emma's cat as she was his. Maybe more. The cat shifted closer to Emma, proving the point. The soft engine of her purring warmed and mingled with the babies' breath. Now he was sure. Whatever Bible Man was, he really had left that night in the snowstorm. Emma and the cat came back. He didn't.

At dinner the next night, Walt pulled Ben out of the high chair and onto his lap, sat back in his chair and said, "Guess what I found out today?"

Rith finished up the last of his potatoes, watching the cat slink around behind the potted plant in the corner.

"You know John Repinski at work," Walt said.

"Yes," said Mom.

"Well his boy Ryan, as it turns out," said Walt, "is a grad student. And guess what he studies?"

"I don't know, Walt," said Mom. "What does he study?"

Rith waited for slack in the conversation so he could ask to be excused.

"Greek!" said Walt, leaning back in his chair. "He studies Greek. And he might have figured out something about your name, Rith."

Rith glanced up as Ben grabbed Walt's lip and yanked on it.

"Hey," said Walt, peeling Ben's fingers off of his face. "Ease up, boy."

"What did you find out?" asked Mom.

"Well, according to Ryan, wait a sec . . ."

He dug in his pocket, pulled out a piece of paper, unfolded it, and read.

"There was a Greek princess named Orithyia. She was

kidnapped by the north wind and there are suggestions that she was a priestess of Bacchus."

"So I'm named after a girl?" Rith asked, any hopes he might have had taking a crash-dive.

"Sort of looks that way," said Walt. "But the *n* on the end, that makes it a boy's name. Like Orion, that hunter guy."

Rith looked at Mom. She shrugged. "That's more than I ever got," she said. "I still don't quite understand it, but it sounds like your name really might be Greek."

"It's all Greek to me," said Walt.

Mom and Rith both looked at him and he smiled, shrugging.

"Sorry, I couldn't resist. Here, take the e-mail. Ryan said if you want to know more maybe he can help you out."

"Can I be excused?" said Rith, taking the paper.

"Sure," said Walt.

He read the paper on the way up the stairs. A princess who got kidnapped by the north wind. So it was a Greek name, but so what? It meant nothing. What could you expect from a guy who hadn't even finished high school?

Rith called Toby and told him the good news/bad news.

"At least I can stop trying to figure it out now," he said. "It's just like my Mom thought, he heard something and probably got it mixed up, or made up his own thing from it."

"Hang on," said Toby. "How do you spell Orithyia? Like yours without the *n?* I want to poke around and see if I can figure out anything else."

178

"Don't bother," said Rith. "I'd rather just forget about it. I gotta go. I've got a bunch of science homework to do."

He was just finishing up the questions at the end of the chaper when Mom knocked on the door.

"Come in," he said, turning.

She sat on the edge of the bed across from him.

"I'm sorry, hon," she said. "I know you were hoping for more than that, but at least it's something. And it was nice of Walt to find that out for you."

"He thought it was funny," said Rith. "All Greek to me, haha, and a princess besides."

"He felt bad about that. He really was trying to help."

"Whatever."

"Don't you whatever me, Orithian. It's been a lot the last few weeks, maybe things can just slow down around here. How's the homework going?"

"Almost done," he said.

"Good. And you know what? Maybe you're the original Orithian, and that's the best way to be."

The phone rang the next morning about five minutes after Rith's alarm went off.

"Rith!" called Mom. "It's for you. It's Toby."

Rith shook himself awake and picked up the phone.

"What's up?" he asked.

"Rith! Dude! I hit the jackpot! I would've called you last night but it was after eleven and Dad said if I did he'd cut me off the computer for five years. Check this out though. You said your dad liked mountains, right?"

"Yeah, so?"

"So I found out that Greek names are made out of putting different words together. And I looked up all these different sites about that goddess and Greek words. And—wait, let me get this right—her name is *oros* and *thyo* and *oros* means mountain."

"For real?"

"Yeah, go online and look for yourself. *Oros,* mountain."

"What about the rest of it?"

"*Thyo,* that one was harder. It's got a whole bunch of meanings."

"So *Oros-Thyo?* That doesn't sound like my name."

"I'm telling you, that's how it works. They put the words together and then add some doodad on the end to make it a name. Yeah Mom, in a minute. I gotta go, Rith. The mountain part is for sure, no question about that. And the other stuff—there's a bunch of it. You gotta look for yourself."

Rith turned on his computer and got into Google. He saw right away what Toby meant. When he put in "thyo greek" he got 177 hits. The first few were about the thymus gland, Lent, and the spice thyme. He had no idea where to start.

"Rith! Breakfast."

He dug into the recycling can and found the printout of Walt's e-mail from r_repinski@yahoo.com. He typed a message and hit *send.*

The school day went on forever and Rith didn't have a

chance to get at a computer. He saw Toby in the cafeteria and told him what he'd sent to the guy at the university.

"Brilliant," said Toby. "We could sit around Googling till we're ninety and still never know which one was right. An expert is exactly what you need."

"I don't know if he's an expert," said Rith. "He's just a student."

"That's more of an expert than either of us."

After school, Rith dashed upstairs and turned the computer on. He had mail.

*Hi Orithian. Your friend is right, the name Orithyia is from **oros** (mountain) and **thyo** . . . and there are plenty of interpretations for what **thyo** might mean. One source says that her name means "mountain rusher" or one who storms, rushes, or rages on the mountain. **Thyo** commonly means sacrifice but originally it meant an intense movement of air, water, ground, smoke, animals, or men. And **thymos** is vital force or spirit. So I think you can pick any of those and they'd be right. Mountain rusher, mountain storm, mountain spirit or force, or mountain sacrifice (you might not want that one) and no Greek scholar is going to tell you you're wrong. If you have more questions let me know. RR.*

Rith blinked hard, staring at the screen. The words blurred and he blinked again. There was the meaning, objectively and in fact. A Greek scholar said so.

He pulled the picture out of his Bible, the one of him and his dad at Mount Rock, and held it up to the screen in front of the e-mail message. That guy right there named him. The guy who talked about climbing mountains but never even went out of the state until he flew to Florida to drive a van full of cocaine back to Minnesota. The guy who pretended to be dead so he wouldn't have to face his kid. He hadn't heard the name from somebody in a bar and gotten it wrong and then lied about it. He had named his son Orithian, a name that was true and real, objectively and in fact.

"Rith, I didn't hear you come in."

Rith jumped, startled.

"What's this, you don't even say hello to your mother anymore?"

"Mom," he said, his voice shaking. "Come here and look at this."

She came in, Ben in her arms and Emma trailing behind. "What is it?"

"This. This e-mail. It's from that guy, the one Walt knows."

She stood behind him to read, inhaled sharply, then let it out with a soft "Oh."

"You remember the first time you took me to that climbing wall at REI?" Rith said, and his voice shook completely out of control. "Climbing it felt like that. I don't know, it's hard to explain. Like I just had to rush it, all the way up."

Mom set Ben down on the floor and spun Rith's chair

so he faced her.

"Orithian," she said, her eyes soft and swimming. Emma stood with a couple of fingers in her mouth and stared. Mom put her hands on his knees and looked him deep in the eye. Tears spilled all over her cheeks and he felt one trickle down his own.

"He got it right," she said, nodding. "He got it exactly right."

Rith was awake in the night again. The cat hadn't woken him and neither had his alarm. He was just awake. He walked down the stairs, feeling the carpet beneath his bare feet, fine with that. Wooden stairs or not, he'd been called by name. By his own father.

He sat on the leather couch in the living room, facing the blank TV screen. The cat meowed and Rith spotted her in the doorway to the nursery.

"Hey kitty," Rith said. "Wanna come sit with me?"

She padded across the carpet and leapt up onto the couch, settling in next to him. If only Bible Man would show up too. Rith traced his fingertip from the cat's nose to the soft fur between her ears and down the length of her spine. She was warm and solid and breathing. Reality. A door opened and the cat sat up, then jumped across to the coffee table.

"Rith?" Walt's shape filled the hallway. "Is that you?"

"Yeah, it's me," said Rith.

"I thought I heard someone up. Are the kids okay?"

"I don't know, probably."

The shape faded back into the shadows, and Rith imagined him going into the nursery, checking the crib and the bed. Walt came back out and sat in the over-stuffed chair, putting his feet on the coffee table.

"What are you doing up?" asked Walt.

"Nothing."

The cat looked over at Walt and meowed.

"Doesn't look like anyone's going to claim Kitty," said Walt.

"No," said Rith, leaning forward to gently flick a velvet ear. "I think she's ours."

"Fine by me," said Walt. "I like her. Are we going to keep calling her Kitty?"

"Might as well," said Rith. "She's used to it now."

The cat hopped over to the couch and settled next to Rith again, purring. As he stroked her, Rith could almost hear the crackling fire. How strange, to have Walt sitting there with him and the cat in the Bible Man Zone.

"Speaking of names," said Walt. "Good detective work, you and Toby. Mountain Rusher, that's good. I'm glad Ryan could help."

"Yeah, thanks for that."

As Rith continued to stroke the length of the cat, she turned up the volume of her purr.

"We could call her Jag," said Walt. "She sounds like a perfectly tuned Jaguar. Plus it's a double meaning, you know, cat and car."

"Nah," said Rith. "Emma's going to call her Kitty no matter what we say."

"Yeah," laughed Walt. "Once Emma gets stuck on something, that's the way it is."

Rith ran a finger under the cat's throat, feeling the motor of her voice box beneath the skin. She leaned her head out, then dipped her ear down to rub against his palm.

"So Walt," said Rith. "I was thinking. Toby's going to try some other churches. What if I went with him sometimes?"

The cat's motor rose and fell with her breath while Rith waited for Walt to say no.

"I made a promise," Walt said. "When you got baptized. It was a promise to God. I promised to raise you in a Christian household, to make sure you learn about the Christian faith and go to worship services."

"Can't I get learn from other places too? At least sometimes? Seems like the faith thing should be my choice, unless you just want to make me go until you can't make me anymore."

"Let me think about it and talk about it with your mom. Or maybe Pastor Paul."

"He'll say no," said Rith.

"Maybe. But he's not the one who decides in the end. Your mom and I are."

Was Walt really less Waltish since the nickel thing? Or had Rith been a fool all along, just like Bible Man said? Lying lips and slander and all. Rith rubbed behind the cat's ear and she made the soft squeaky sound, dream-kitty language for "go ahead and ask."

"You know that whole thing about adopting me?" he asked. "Why bother? It's expensive, right? With a lawyer and all?"

"Well, it would mean that you're automatically considered my son, equal with Ben and Emma, if I die. I don't have to put special provisions in my will about you. You just get the goods."

Walt waited for a response but Rith didn't give him one.

"And if something happened to your mom, I'd be your legal guardian. Nobody would question it."

Rith hadn't thought about that before. What if Mom died? What would happen to him?

"That's not really it, though," said Walt. "Those things. Because those things we could fix anyway, legally. I used to think that if I could make you my son, things would be different. I'd understand you more, maybe you'd like me more."

He gave out a short, barky laugh.

"Like maybe if I could say you were my son, legally, then everything would be easier. I guess that wasn't the smartest thing I ever came up with."

The cat rolled over and grabbed Rith's hand with her front paws. No claws, just soft round pads gently batting his fingers. *In an abundance of counselors there is safety.* Bible Man couldn't have meant Walt, could he?

The silence was thick and loud until Rith broke it.

"Well, maybe it's not the dumbest thing you ever came up with, either," he said.

The thickness dissolved and the new silence was a quiet one. Just as Rith's eyelids began to grow heavy, the cat made a loud muttering noise. She rolled out from under Rith's hand and jumped across to the table.

"I guess that's our cue," said Walt. "Time for bed."

His hulking shape unfolded and rose from the chair.

"Good night," he said.

He walked around the furniture, knocking an end table as he went, and disappeared into the shadows of the hall.

Rith stayed where he was, watching the silhouette of the cat in the darkness. She sat perfectly still and watched him back. Then she meeped and looked at the stairs. Rith could almost hear the raspy voice in the darkness.

"Go up in peace to your house," it would say.

He did.

About the Author

Pat Schmatz grew up in rural Wisconsin and still lives in the woods of her childhood. Over the years, she has supported her writing habit with a variety of jobs, including forklift operator, janitor, fitness consultant, stable hand, secretary, and shipping clerk.

Pat Schmatz was a fiscal year 2003 recipient of a fellowship grant from the Minnesota State Arts Board. This work is made possible in part by a grant from the Minnesota State Arts Board, through an appropriation by the Minnesota State Legislature and a grant from the National Endowment for the Arts.